Remember Me

Other Titles by S G Miles, Writing as Geoffrey Lewis:
The D.I. David Russell Crime Novels:

Cycle	978-0-9545624-3-4
Flashback	978-0-9545624-0-3
Strangers	978-0-9545624-1-0
Winter's Tale	978-0-9545624-2-7
Gameboy	978-0-9564536-5-5

The Michael Baker Canal Trilogy:

A Boy Off The Bank	978-0-9545624-6-5
A Girl At The Tiller	978-0-9545624-7-2
The New Number One	978-0-9545624-8-9
Cattle & Sheep & Boats	978-0-9564536-3-1

The Jess Carter Children's Canal Stories:

Jess Carter & The Oil Boat	978-0-9564536-1-7
Jess Carter & The Bolinder	978-0-9564536-2-4
Jess Carter & The Rodneys	978-0-909551-00-8

Other Canal Stories:

Starlight   978-0-9545624-5-8

And:

Thunderchild   978-0-9551900-6-3

Being the first part of the Lord of the Storm fantasy trilogy, published 2010.

Also:

L-Plate Boating (with Tom McManus)
978-0-9564536-0-0

For more information please go to:
www.sgmpublishing.co.uk

Remember Me
and other stories

S G Miles

About the Author:

Stephen Miles was born in Oxford, in 1947. Educated at the city's High School, and subsequently at Hatfield Polytechnic (now a University), he pursued a varied career including periods as a research chemist, a professional photographer and a security guard.

After many years in the motor trade, he finally spent eight years as owner and captain of a passenger trip-boat on the Grand Union Canal. His writing began during this time, at first as a way of filling in the dark winter days when his seasonal business was in the doldrums. His first book, *Flashback,* was published in 2003, under his pen-name of Geoffrey Lewis – he now has a total of ten novels and four children's books in print, with many more planned in the coming years!

Remember Me is the first volume to include some of his short stories; an addition to the famous Michael Baker trilogy is now in print, along with the third Jess Carter book. The second part of his 'Lord of the Storm' fantasy trilogy is also completed, and will be published in due course. Canal boater, amateur photographer and American car enthusiast, he now lives in Milton Keynes where he enjoys a pint of 'proper' beer...

Copyright © Stephen G. Miles 2013

S G Miles has asserted his right under the Copyrights, Designs and Patents Act 1998 to be identified as the author of this work.

All Rights Reserved.
No part of this publication may be reproduced, stored in a retrieval system, or transmitted in any form or by any means, mechanical, photocopying, recording or otherwise, without the prior written permission of the publisher.

This book is a work of fiction. Any resemblance of the characters to actual people, or of the events described to actual occurrences, is entirely coincidental.

ISBN 978-1-909551-22-0

First Published in 2013 by:

SGM Publishing
47 Silicon Court, Shenley Lodge, Milton Keynes
MK5 7DJ
info@sgmpublishing.co.uk
07792-497116

Introduction

Greetings, dear reader. I'm delighted to welcome you to this first collected volume of what I might describe as bits and pieces of my writing!

I have never considered myself to be a writer of short stories – many successful writers begin that way, but it wasn't so for me. I began, from the first, with full-length novels, publishing my first crime story in 2003 – as I write this intro, I have ten novels in print, and three children's books, with a fourth in preparation. For me, the idea of short stories came later – over the last year or two, in fact. The short stories in this volume have all been written in that period, each inspired by some simple thing that has triggered my over-active imagination!

People often ask where I get the inspiration for my stories. My historical canal tales all grew out of my own love of England's waterways, and my fascination with the lives of those amazing families who lived and worked in the narrowboats of what is now a bygone era. But each of the stories in this book I can trace back to a single moment when something set up an echo in my mind - take the first story, for example: *Coming Home* doesn't have any specific location mentioned, but it was inspired by a walk in Jubilee Country Park, in Petts Wood, Kent, with my teenage nephew and one of his schoolfriends. I noticed the imprint of bicycle tyres in the dried-out puddles of the pathways in the park, and that set up the train of thought which became the story you read here. *Starlight,* both the initial passage reproduced here and the eventual novel which was published some years ago, grew out of a line of dialogue in a feature film which struck a similar chord – and so on.

The central story in this book, *Remember Me,* was similarly inspired by a line from a popular song, and the Australian setting felt right from the very first. I have a deep love of Australia – my older sister emigrated there many years ago, and my only regret is that it took me until 2006 to make the trip there to visit her and see the country for myself. Kananga Station and township are, of course, fictional, but the other locations mentioned are all real – I have stayed in Roma, where my sister's children grew up, and walked along Main Street in Mitchell, and stood beside a dirt-track road with nothing between me and the horizon but red soil and stunted bush trees. It is an amazing country – the outback of Queensland awesome in its dry immensity, with a harsh but stunning beauty that you have to experience to appreciate. Perhaps my feelings will come across in the words of Cobbo, and of young Jack Westrom.

I can perhaps best describe *Remember Me,* if I can use the word in a Shakespearean sense, as a tragedy. I hope that term won't put you off, my dear reader – it hasn't done our Will too much harm over the centuries! But it is, in fairness, a rather sad little tale – as, in their own way, are the short stories which accompany it. Most of them do include a twist, an uplift which relieves the sadness – and perhaps the closing scene of *Remember Me* does the same in its own fashion, a reminder that life always goes on, that joy and humour can at last lift the shadows however dark they may seem.

In the case of *Remember Me,* I must acknowledge a lot of help in getting the background of the story right: My thanks go to the staff and volunteers of the Jondaryan Woolshed in Queensland, who gave of their knowledge of the wool trade and the round of life on an outback sheep station. And most especially to my niece, who grew up in Roma and knew the outback life and ways from her childhood – from her came much of the detail which helps to give the authenticity to my tale.

So it is that this book is dedicated,
with my thanks and my love:

to Byn.

Contents

Coming Home	11
Remember Me	23
In The Snow	151
Graduation Day	159
Starlight (original draft)	171

Coming Home

The park hasn't changed much over the years. The trees are taller than I remember, and one or two of the footpaths have been gravelled now where they were bare earth then; the old wooden benches that dotted the paths have been replaced with modern ones, rather more of them now as well. And the little pond, that was a kid's delight in its wilderness, has been 'improved' into a neat and tidy sanitised spot with its own benches and picnic tables.

As I wander along, just following my feet, I'm on familiar territory – familiar from so long ago, not seen for so many years. And as I walk, my mind is lost in the past, back in those days long hidden in the depth of my memory, when my whole world had fallen apart...

I had walked this way then, one day when all the fuss was over and done, when that awful sense of anti-climax had taken over, when I had had to face the beginning of the rest of my life. I could not then, nor can I now, ever remember being there alone before – and that aloneness was threatening to crush my heart, to stop the breath in my throat and burn out my eyes with tears.

We had been there together, just the week before, enjoying the sunshine after a heavy spring shower. We were on our bicycles, and I was following him – that was how my life had been, always in his footsteps, following behind, looking up, admiring, worshipping...

The puddles we had splashed through, the water sparkling in the sunlight as it sprayed from our wheels as bright as our laughter, as joyful as the grin on his face as he'd looked over his shoulder at me, had dried out now, the soft mud at their bottoms bearing the imprint of shoes – and the tracks of bicycle tyres. I stopped, gazing down, remembering, wondering, fancying I could tell which had been the tracks of his tyres – there! Those tyres with the squarish tread, his were like that... I knew, even then, that my thoughts were fanciful, but it made me feel, just for a moment, close to him again to imagine that I could tell where he had been, to detect, somehow, his past presence in that hard, dried mud. I went from puddle to puddle, remembering the way we had gone, following our tracks whether they were real or imagined.

We had circled the pond, outside its surrounding stand of old willow trees, and then dropped our bikes to push in under their deep cover. The waters had been dark then, shaded even in the sunshine by their overhanging branches, the kind of place that any kid delighted in. We accepted that all of the local kids knew it, and went there frequently, but still it felt like our own secret place – we would go there to just be together, to sit and talk or fool around. If others were there when we arrived, we might join them, or turn away and go somewhere else, depending on our mood.

That day, I had found myself standing there, peering under the trees from outside, imagining that if I was to push through under them to the water's edge I would find him there, laughing, telling me it had all been a big mistake. It seemed that I could hear his voice, calling to me as it had so many times before:

'Come on Drew – what are you waiting for?' Hoping against hope, knowing that nothing but heartbreak awaited me, I had thrust my way into the undergrowth, only to find myself even more alone. And then my aloneness had overwhelmed me, risen like a black tide, submerging me beneath waves of grief and fear, fear of being alone for the rest of my life. I sat down on a fallen tree-trunk, where we used to sit together, and buried my face in my hands and wept. I cried for my loneliness, of course – but I cried for him too, for the life he would never know, for the future he would never see.

I never knew how long I sat there, lost in my sorrow and hopelessness. It had been after a silent, tasteless lunch that I had left the house; the evening was drawing in when my mother found me and gently took me home.

But home wasn't home any more. Or perhaps it just wasn't mine any more. The rooms looked the same, the furniture hadn't changed, or the decoration – my toys were where I'd left them, my clothes in the drawers where they should be. But the door to his room was closed as it had never been, and the absence of his voice weighed upon me like a heavy blanket of silence killing all the sound in the world.

Home had always been a place of joy, of noise and laughter, the four of us together in shared love and harmony. I won't pretend that we were perfect kids – we both got things wrong, got told off from time to time, but that did nothing to upset the warmth that surrounded us. But in the last week that warmth had vanished as though it had never been; home had become a cold, silent place, a place of darkness where no-one spoke unless they had to.

My mother tried, God bless her! Looking back now, I can see just how hard she tried, burying her own grief to try to soften mine, fighting to lift my father out of the deep depression he had sunk into, fighting, as I realise now, to save her marriage and her life. That she failed in both was hardly her fault – Dear God how she tried! It was more than a year before she gave up, before the silence and the darkness finally got to her and she took me and walked out. That saved her life, I am quite certain, getting away from the atmosphere of guilt and horror that had come to permeate our world and having me to focus her love and care upon, to the exclusion of her own sorrow. But it didn't save her in the end – the breast cancer that took her from me ten years later may not have resulted from her stress over all those years, but it did nothing to help her resilience, weakening her resistance, taking away, when it came to it, her will to live.

And my father. Now, with the blessing of hindsight, I can dimly understand what he was going through. At ten years old though, all I could see was my own grief and a man who had been my friend, who could hardly bear to look at me any more. Now I can begin to see the depth of his pain, to feel, even at secondhand, what he must have felt – not only the intense sorrow but the knowledge that he had been responsible for the death of his first-born son. And he knew, too, that in my childish grief and anger, I blamed him as well. I hadn't held back from telling him so, when my agony got the better of me before the funeral, hitting him with my fists, yelling at him until my mother pulled me away. I hadn't wanted to see the tears streaming down his face then; I needed to blame someone for my brother, my best friend, my hero, being gone from my side – and he was the one in the line of fire.

He'd been so proud of that car. I can still see the look on his face when he got out of it after driving it home, grinning from ear to ear:

'Tom! Drew! Come and see!' We'd been waiting to hear him draw up, and were out of the door almost before he could call us. We gazed at it in wonder, walking around it, touching it, running our hands over the clean, beautiful curves of its bodywork, peering inside at the slim leather seats, eyes wide at the instrument panel that looked as if it belonged in a jet fighter. He opened the bonnet, and our mouths dropped open at the sight of the big six-cylinder engine, all gleaming polished aluminium and black enamel. He had been saving for a car like this for as long as I could remember, promising us we would have one one day – a real E-Type Jaguar, a 1962 fixed-head coupe in a rich dark blue, the seats covered in light tan leather.

'Dad – can we go out in it? Let's take it for a run! Can we?' Tom was as excited as he was.

'Yeah, why not? Who's coming first?'

'Let's all go – please Dad!' I didn't want to be left behind.

'Whoa – it's only got two seats, Drew!' Tom peered into the back through the window in the luggage hatch:

'Someone could sit in the back, Dad, there's plenty of room!' He looked from one to the other of us, and then nodded:

'Okay, then. Drew – you're the smallest, you get into the back.'

'No, Dad, I'll go in the back.' My brother turned to me: 'You have the seat, Drew – you've got a safety belt then. Just in case!' He laughed, taking away the seriousness of his words, and then climbed over the seats into the luggage space. I didn't argue, but sat proudly in the passenger seat once he was settled behind me. Dad got in again behind the wheel; the engine started with a deep growl that had us thrilling to its sound, and then we were off, Mum waving from the front door.

We went out into the country, along the quiet lanes, my father driving fast but carefully despite the two of us both urging him on:

'Go on Dad! Faster!' The Jag was a fabulous car, so powerful, so agile, or at least that was how it felt to us, riding in it. It had been raining again that morning, but still it went around the bends as if it was on rails. Turning back towards home, we came to a small crossroads; he threw it into the turn, stepping on the throttle again to drive around the corner – but the back wheels let go, and we were sliding sideways across the road. He tried to correct the skid, but one back wheel hit the raised curb with a tremendous jolt, throwing me hard against the door; he fought the car to a halt, and looked around:

'You okay, Drew?' I nodded shakily, nursing a bruised shoulder, and he looked behind us:

'Tom – Tom?' He reached over, shaking him by the shoulder: 'Tom – Tom!' I saw the horror in his eyes: 'TOM!' He was screaming my brother's name now, but Tom just lay there, unmoving.

I had been badly shaken by the shunt, my body bruised by the safety belt. Tom had been kneeling on the luggage platform, his arms resting on the backs of our seats, gazing through the windscreen as we'd hurtled along the narrow roads; when the tyre hit the curb, he'd been thrown sideways against the window. His neck was broken – that was what they told us later.

There's a fallacy that it offers some kind of comfort to be told that someone you love has died instantly, that they didn't suffer. Believe me, it is no comfort at all when the one person who has lit up your life since the day you were born suddenly isn't there any more. And beneath my pain was my own sense of guilt – if I hadn't given in to his suggestion, if I'd made him sit in the front, he would still have been alive. I would have been the one who died, and it seemed to my young self that that would have been a much fairer outcome.

Another platitude: It is better to have loved and lost... Is it? If he had never been born, I would have lived my life in comfort, in the warmth of my family, never knowing what I had missed. But he had been my big brother, my idol, the sun that warmed my world, and I had loved him with a love that had made my heart ache – but now my heart was broken, shattered, scattered like ashes over my world.

But if I was in pain, how much worse was my father's agony? I may not have wanted to know then, but now I can see how he was suffering. It's a cliche maybe, but from the moment that he realised Tom was badly hurt, he was broken, finished. He never touched the Jag again – it was collected by the garage, taken away, and we never saw it again. The ironic thing is that it was not even scratched – just the tyre that had burst as it hit the curb. He went back to work after the funeral, but it was only going through the motions – all of his ambition was gone, the zest for life that had kept us all close through my first ten years vanished as if it had never been. I must bear some responsibility for his pain, too – I had made no bones about blaming him for Tom's death, and he understood, I know, just how much my brother had meant to me, how much his loss was hurting me. So his guilt carried over into feeling responsible for my grief as well – it's hardly surprising that he felt estranged from me, couldn't even look at me unless he had to. The very sight of me must have driven home to him over and again just what he had lost, what a simple, silly mistake had cost all of us.

He's gone too, now. I'm the only one left. He never moved, stayed in the house we had all shared in those long-gone days of our joy and happiness. He stayed in the same job, took the same train into the City every day, frequented the same shops, walked the same streets. And wandered in the same park where he had sometimes come with us to play, chasing us through the trees or kicking a ball around on the grass.

I turn my footsteps homewards. Homewards? That is a word I haven't thought of in connection with that house for over thirty years. It's mine now, of course – I am his sole beneficiary, so I own it, lock, stock and barrel. I haven't seen it in all that time, never returned after Mum and I left; earlier, I had wandered through the silent, empty rooms, alone again, tears in my eyes, hearing across the years the echo of my brother's voice, the sound of his laughter.

Back along the paths, out through 'our' gate into the road. Cross over, down the sidestreet; through the narrow alley where we used to pedal furiously, hoping no old lady would appear at the far end to make us slow down. Out again, turn left; around the corner, six houses down, and I turn into the drive where my car stands. The gate into the garden stands open, and I walk up to it, looking through. He never even took down the goalpost where Tom and I used to imagine we were playing for the Arsenal – the net is long gone, but that isn't stopping the two boys taking turns to shoot penalties at each other.

I feel as though my heart is going to burst as I watch them. Yes, I know now the agony my father suffered all those years ago, the pain he lived with all through the thirty-odd years since. How would I feel if anything happened to either of these boys? How especially if it was my own fault? He may have, in all truth, been to blame, but at last I can find it in me to forgive my father, to sympathise with him. It's too late to tell him so, but I hope that maybe he can still understand, and know that I did love him, in spite of everything.

One of the boys spots me, beckons me to join them:

'Come on Dad! You're in goal!'

'Whoa, Tom, I need a rest and a cup of tea.'

'Oh Dad! You've been gone for *ages!*' Ben protests too. They both come over to me; Tom has the football in his hands. I put an arm around each of them, kiss each in turn on their tousled heads:

'Just a quick cuppa, okay? Then I'll come out here with you.' The kitchen door at my side opens:

'It's a good thing I've got the kettle on then, is it?' Sophie stands in the doorway grinning at us.

'Thanks, love. Then I suppose I'll have to risk life and limb with these two monsters!'

We all crowd into the kitchen while she brews and pours the tea:

'Dad?'

'Yes, Tom?'

'This is your house too, as well as ours? I mean, as well as where we live?'

'That's right. Your grandad left it to me when he died.'

'Can we come and live here then? It's much bigger, and the garden's *wicked!* I know it's a bit overgrown, but Mum'll soon sort that out!' Sophie gives him an amused look, her eyebrows raised, but she says nothing as Ben chimes in:

'Yes, Dad, please Dad! It'd be *brilliant!*'

'We'll think about it, okay?' The decision had already been made – subject to their reaction to the place on this first visit, anyway - but we weren't going to tell them that: 'Suppose we do – who's having which bedroom?' They look at each other, and then dash from the kitchen, their footsteps clattering up the stairs, their voices echoing through the empty rooms.

I look at Sophie, and I know that she knows what is in my heart – with the sound of children's laughter ringing through it, this old house *can* be a home again.

I'm coming home.

Remember Me

The old homestead of the Kananga Station stands derelict today. Rooms where generations have lived, laughed and loved lie empty and silent, daylight creeping through gaps in the rotten iron of the roof, and dust lining the bare boards where so many feet have trod. In the spacious kitchen which has seen so many parties – Christmases, birthdays, weddings, anniversaries – the big oak table too is streaked with dust, and the sun has dried the wood to a dull grey, and split it across in several places. The iron wood-burning range too is cracked and derelict, its flue broken. Little has been disturbed in many years, except for the incursions of exploring dingoes, the scurrying of rats, and the pattering of insects.

More than thirty years have passed since the 33,000 acres of Kananga were incorporated into the neighbouring property. The economics of wool production and lamb farming may have been partly to blame – but in the end, it came down to its widowed owner, who finally gave up the unequal struggle to maintain what her husband and his antecedents had built up. The owner of Worrongatta then was only too happy to buy her out – and the bank too could see the potential of a bigger holding – so in the end it came down to simply following the line of least resistance.

But one day last autumn, all that dust and the echoing silence were disturbed. Around mid-day, an electric blue Ford Utility turned onto the track which led the half-mile from the main road to the house, and drew up outside the bunkhouse. The engine died, the door opened, and a man stepped out. An elderly man, tall and rangy, his face lined and weatherbeaten, his bushy hair grey now, thinning on top where his scalp was protected by an old Akubra hat. His check shirt and jeans were worn but clean, his boots equally tired but polished; a light jacket hung loose over his shoulders.

He stood there, the high sun warming his broad back, looking at the abandoned house. A feeling of melancholy rose in his mind at its derelict state as he took in the dry and flaking paint, the corroded, slightly sunken corrugated tin of the roof, but a slight smile touched his lips as he recalled the way it used to be. Built in traditional Queenslander style, its stout wooden structure still stood high on robust stumps, clear of the ground in order to allow cooling air to circulate beneath, and to slow the questing snakes and white ants down – the all-around veranda still shaded the sides. Behind the main house, the big separate kitchen had lost the covered walkway which had led to the back door but looked otherwise sound even if its roof slumped broken and collapsed, the timbers ravaged by termites.

He walked over to the kitchen door, hanging from one hinge, and peered within:

'Halloo!' His loud call was only a gesture, and he knew it; with the continuing silence, he stepped inside and looked around. Overhead, daylight streamed through the rusted tin roof leaving a pattern like sunshine on a forest floor over boards and table, twinkling on some broken glass. Turning, he wandered across the few yards of open space and through the abandoned house, memories running through his mind – the sound of voices, the turn of a smile, the laughter of a child...

He stepped out into the daylight again, lifted his face to the sky where light clouds drifted slowly between wide horizons, and looked around. Some of the buildings and equipment looked to be still in use – the shearing shed and the bunkhouse, presumably occupied for those few weeks of frenetic activity once a year – the old windmill stood still and silent now, but in good repair, ready to pump water up from the bore as and when it might be needed. He strolled around behind the shearing shed, and smiled – the old generator was gone from its own little shack: *They must bring one in for shearing, nowadays.* The paddocks too showed signs of recent maintenance, the fences strong and sound; so too were the big holding sheds, leading him to the conclusion that the station's facilities were still used every year even if no-one lived there any more. It would make some sense, perhaps – a large station, covering a big acreage – less distance to have to muster the sheep, rather than having to herd the mobs to one shed which might be way off at the other end of the land.

He walked slowly back to the nearly-new Falcon and opened the door. He stood there, looking around him: *So where are you? What happened?* He was a man who had spent his life since childhood moving on, going from one place to another, one job to another, so the absence of those he had come to seek did not trouble him too much: *Did you sell out after all, Angie? You spoke of it sometimes, even then...*

He knew his quest was far from over. Rural Queensland is a place of continuity, of stability and longevity. There would be people around still who had known them, who had known him, even, from so many years ago. People who would know where they had gone, who could tell him where he should go next to find them. Maybe it would be a long trail, but he didn't care; he would follow it to its end, wherever that might take him, however many days, weeks, months it might take. Even years. It was just a question of where to try first.

But as he stood there in the Ute's open door, pondering the next move in his search, he found himself assailed by memories, and a growing sense of regret. *They were happy times, weren't they?* Perhaps even the happiest times in his long life. He gazed around, remembering, picturing the scene as it had been, hearing the sounds of life where now there was only an empty silence. And with the memories came a mood of reflection: *I guess I've had a good life, mostly – but I've made plenty of mistakes along the way. Was that the biggest of them all? Why – why did I ever leave this place, these people?*

In his heart, he knew the answer. Wanderlust had possessed him since childhood, led him to run away at fourteen, and guided his feet ever since – and it had taken more than sixty years since then to convince him that there was nothing to fear in the demon of commitment, the awful prospect of giving up a part of his life to another, of loving, and allowing himself to be loved in return. Had that yearning for the far horizon been reason enough for his going? Had his fear of being tied down been reason enough to walk away, to turn his back on a woman he'd respected and admired, on a child who had – he shamed himself into admitting it at last – grown to love him? *Oh Jack! Jacko-boy...*

But now, the decision was made. After a lifetime of hard work and wandering, he was coming home – wherever home might be! *Where are you now, Jacko?* Who *are you? You'll be a fine man, I know that much – nearing fifty, now! What did you do with your life? I'm coming, boy – maybe you'll be angry with me still, maybe you'll turn me away, and if you do I know it's what I deserve. But if you loved me then, perhaps you can still. And your mother – is she still alive? Is she with you, wherever you are?*

He forced his mind back to the present, shaking his head with a rueful smile: *Stop day-dreaming and get on with it, or you'll turn up your toes before you ever get there!* So – the next step? Worrongatta? The neighbouring station's house stood about twenty miles away, over the horizon to the west: *Did you sell out to the Millers, Angie? Old man Miller always wanted to combine Kananga with his property, didn't he?* He lowered himself into the driving seat, started the engine and drove off down the track to the main road, where he braked the truck to a halt and turned his head, looking both ways. If she had sold to the Millers, they would be able to point the way forward for him – but maybe they'd gone too? He smiled to himself, shook his head and turned back the way he had come – first stop, the fount of all local knowledge anywhere in the outback. The nearest pub.

***

Kananga Township lies out in the open bush, away to the north-west of Roma, clustered around the point where the

Kananga Creek is crossed by an old drover's road. As a centre of population, it is insignificant to the point of vanishment – a small garage; a general store which will supply you with a range of provisions, a nut and bolt, or a new tractor; the Kananga Inn, with its popular bar and a few rooms to let for those foolhardy enough to want to stay there; a couple more shops, a bank (open Wednesdays and Fridays) and a few houses. Like many outback towns, it exists for little else than to provide supplies and services - and, in the case of the pub, recreation – for the properties which surround it.

Today, many of these combine the running of both cattle and sheep, the production of beef as well as lamb and wool. And tourism – the growing fashion for outback holidays, a week or two spent staying in a 'real bush station' demands owners who will offer such hospitality and facilities to both Australian and foreign visitors. And the Kananga district can offer a taste of the outback, while being within reasonable reach of Queensland's two major cities, Brisbane and Toowoomba.

The main road which the old man followed back from the station even today runs out of tarmac at the town limits, to become little more than a dirt track, sometimes to become impassable in the rains of summer. The Ute purred back into town, the old man looking around him, smiling as he realised how little the place had changed. There were a few more houses now, another street turning off where there had been wild scrub back in the 1970s; the main store had a bright new frontage, and there was a new cafe where the little bakers had been back in his day. He drove slowly along the main street, paused outside the general store looking at the dusty Toyota four-wheel-drive parked there, but then went on and swung around to pull up next to a shiny Jeep in front of the Kananga Inn...

It was many hours later, as the evening drew in around the little town, when the old man made his way wearily up the stairs from the bar to the room he had taken for the next two nights. He might decide to stay longer before he moved on again, but for now, he needed to be alone. Alone with his thoughts and his memories.

Since his arrival in the pub, many of his questions had been answered; and it seemed that a lot more of the answers might lie within the old school exercise book, in its tired manila envelope, which he carried in his hand. The meeting with Johnny Miller had left him feeling tired and drained – but at least he knew now where to look for those he had come to find.

Dusk had spread its shadows across the bush outside, and the last rays of the sun struck through the spinifex and the dry grasses, the stunted and ungainly gums, beyond the windows of the room at the Kananga Inn. The old man laid his battered suitcase on the bed, and sat down wearily beside it; he looked at the manila envelope in his hand as if half-afraid of what it might contain. He put it down, and slipped out of his light jacket, kicked off his worn boots. Standing up, he ran his fingers through his thinning hair, and then cracked open the stubbie of beer the barman had given him as he passed the bar. He took a long draft of the cool liquid, and then looked down at the envelope again.

He sat down on the bed, his eyes still on the innocent, grubby manila. *He would want you to have it* – Johnny Miller's words echoed in his mind, but still he fought shy of opening it, of reading whatever the aged notebook said: *Come on Cobbo, yeh're tough old Digger, what's got you so scared now?* He reached out and picked the envelope up, opened the already-slit end and tipped out its contents – just as Miller had said, a worn school exercise book, its red cover a little faded after the years. He took the book in his hands and turned it over – on the front, in boyish printed capitals, he read:

THE THOUGHTS OF JACK WESTROM, AGE 13
MARCH 17TH 1976

Something snagged at his heart. He shook his head, half-amused, half-annoyed at his own display of uncharacteristic nervousness, and opened the book...

Hello Diary. Well, this isn't really a diary, but I didn't know how else to start writing. It's just my thoughts, I guess – mum said it might help if I talked about things, about him, way back when he left, but I couldn't. Not then. But now – I still can't talk to her, or anyone, even my friends – but maybe I can talk to you, write it all down, and maybe that'll help.

The script was childish, but neat and rounded. And suddenly, seeing it, he was lost in his memory – looking down, not at the scruffy handwritten page, but into the freckled face of a young boy, laughing blue eyes below a thatch of shaggy, sun-bleached blond hair, a sheet of paper covered in that same neat writing in his hand:

'Here, Cobbo! My history essay, for school – what do yeh think?'

Overcome by the past, he laid the book face-down on the bed and closed his eyes, unable to read on...

It was full dark beyond the windows, the night well on its journey to the morrow's dawn, before the old man picked up the notebook again. He'd long finished the stubbie and trekked downstairs for a couple more:

'You all right, mate? Yeh look shattered!' He'd reassured the younger man who'd taken over the bar since he arrived and trudged back up to his room, neither wanting nor needing any company. The exercise book still lay open where he'd dropped it; stretching out on his back, his head pillowed against the wall at the head of the bed, he picked it up again, almost gingerly: *Come on Cobbo! You've got to read it – if nothin' else, you owe it Jack to see what he had to say.* He opened the book again and began to read...

Hello Diary. Well, this isn't really a diary, but I didn't know how else to start writing. It's just my thoughts, I guess – Mum said it might help if I talked about things, about him, way back when he left, but I couldn't. Not then. But now – I still can't talk to her, or anyone, even my friends – but maybe I can talk to you, write it all down, and maybe that'll help.

His name was Cobbo – at least, that's what we all called him, what everyone called him, or so he told us. Mister Farley – I never knew his real Christian name, or if he ever told me, I can't remember! But why am I talking about him in the past? He isn't dead, at least I hope not – and I'm sure I'd know, somehow, if he was.

He's just not here any more – and that's my big problem, I guess.

He turned up at the Inn, the Kananga, in the spring. More than two and a half years ago, now. It was just after Mum had sent O'Riley packing, after she'd caught him fiddling the men's wages, skimming the extra money off for himself – she'd hung on, kept her mouth shut until we'd pretty well finished lambing, but then she let him know what she'd found out. Gave him the choice of getting out there and then or talking to the police. It left us tight for help, but it was the lull before shearing then - and just when we needed it, this guy turned up looking for work, and a bed to go with it, he said! Mrs Madden, who was running the Inn then, sent him out to us, and Mum took him on straight away, although he insisted that he didn't want to be manager. But that's what he was, in all but name – at least, after he'd been here a while. Mum took all the decisions, for a bit, but then she soon started to leave things to him, and everything worked out real fine.

I'd just turned eleven, then – my birthday's in September. I remember the first time I saw him – he rolled up in this battered old Holden ute, and kind of stretched his way out of it, cramming a dirty old bush hat on his head. I was sitting under the veranda, beside the front door, reading — I've always enjoyed reading. Just as well, I guess, there isn't too much else to do around here except for work! We've got a wireless, but a lot of the programmes are rubbish, although there are a few things I like to listen to — and the two-way radio of course. Sometimes Mum lets me use it to chat with my mates, like Johnny Miller on the next-door property, and I use it for my school work, with the School of the Air.

Anyway, this guy walks over to me and puts his hand out. I'm not used to grown-ups shaking my hand, like I was their own age, so I was a bit flustered; but I got up and shook hands with him.

'Hi' he says, 'I'm looking for Mrs Westrom?'

'She's in the kitchen' I told him.

'You her son?'

'Yeah — I'm Jack Westrom'

'Pleased to meet you, Jack' he says, 'Can I see your Mum?'

'Sure!' I took him indoors, through the house and out the back; Mum was in the kitchen, getting our dinner.

'Mum? Someone to see you' I said, and she looked around. She rubbed her hands on her apron and held one out to him:

'Hello – I'm Angie Westrom.'

'Hello, Ma'am' he shook her hand: 'They said at the Inn you were in need of some extra hands?'

'Well, I guess so. I've just had to let the manager go – would that be a job to suit you?' He laughed:

'I wouldn't say that I'm manager material, Ma'am, but I'm more'n willin' to work, and help out where I can, if that's any use to you?'

'Well, I'm sure it would be, Mister...?'

'Sorry, Ma'am. Farley – they call me Cobbo. D'you have any space in the bunkhouse?'

'We certainly do, Mr Farley! There's a small room there that Mr O'Riley used to have, you can take that if it'll suit. Rest of the place is pretty full, we've got a good bunch of men here.'

'I'm glad to hear it, Ma'am. I like working with a good crew. They won't take it amiss if I get that room?'

'No – they wouldn't appreciate another body crammed in with them, it's pretty full, like I say!'

'Right-o then. I'll get my swag in there, if it's okay?'

'You go right ahead, Mr Farley.'

'Cobbo, Ma'am, please?' She laughed, not something I remember hearing very often:

'Okay – Cobbo! And I'm Angie.'

'Oh no, Ma'am – you're the boss, you've got to have the respect that deserves. Is it all right if I call you Mrs Westrom?'

'Of course, Cobbo – whatever you're happy with. Have you eaten today?'

'Just a snack, at the pub, a while ago.'

'Casserole of mutton be right for you?'

'I'd never have guessed!' They both laughed, and I joined in as he said: 'That'll do a treat, thank you!'

Cobbo settled in pretty quickly. The other men seemed to take to him with no trouble – if any of them resented the idea that he'd been somehow slipped in over their heads, they never showed it. But he was that kind of fellow – he'd work happily alongside them, on whatever job was in hand at the time – and then, when it was needed, he'd somehow quietly take charge, make sure the right thing was done, but so unobtrusively that no-one seemed to notice what had happened. Like I said before, it wasn't long before Mum was beginning to leave a lot of the day-to-day running of the station to him. And me? I guess I took to him, as well, right from that first day.

Maybe what I've got to say will make a bit more sense if I tell you a bit more about me first, though. I've said already that I was just eleven when he turned up at the door - there was only me and Mum, then, like it had been for quite a while. My Dad had died a long time before, when I was only three - he was out with the men bringing in the sheep for shearing, and something spooked his horse. It reared up, and fell - and Dad was underneath. They got him back to the house and sent for the flying doctor, but it was too late.

I was too young to know what was happening - it sounds awful, but I never really grieved for my father. Oh, I cried at the time, but I think that was mostly just shock, the sudden bustle and commotion and the sight of my Mum in tears. By the time I was old enough to realise what I'd lost, it had all kind of slipped away into the past.

Westroms have owned the Kananga since way back. I'd have to ask Mum, look it up, to find out just how long, but I know my great-grandfather was here before the First World War. My Mum came from Brisbane - she met my Dad when he went there with my grandparents once to a graziers convention. She had a hard time of it, when Dad died, but the Millers were a great help, and we got by. It's not a big place, not like some of the Queensland stations – we've got about 33,000 acres. The shearing shed's got six stands, powered off an old generator with a tired British Lister engine that's been there forever! There's two big holding sheds, so the sheep can dry out before shearing if the rains have started by then, and a couple of fenced paddocks too. And there's our house, a bunkhouse for the men with its own kitchen, stables, sheds and outbuildings around the yard. Mr Miller, Johnny's Dad, has suggested combining the two stations, going into partnership with Mum, and I guess it might happen one day.

Until Cobbo came, I'd not had a lot to do with the other men. Mum kind of discouraged me from being with them, and they treated me like 'just a kid'. They'd talk to me, if they saw me around, but it was just a 'G'day, Jack' or a 'How're yeh goin?' Except for old Samuel – he's a pure-blood aboriginal, and he always fascinated me. I'd go and sit with him around his camp-fire, and listen to his stories of the Dreamtime on many warm summer nights, until

Mum came and chased me off to my bed. She would always talk to him too - a lot of folks don't think much of the blackfellas, I've heard them called 'drunken, lazy savages' and things like that, but they're not, really. Their culture goes back just so _far_ into history - and beyond, I guess.

I learnt a lot from Samuel - not just his stories, he showed me how to make a boomerang, and how to throw it! Not that I was any good - I could throw his and have it come back to me, more or less, but the one I tried to make was pretty hopeless. And I learnt how to use a spear, and a woomera - that's the throwing stick they use to give their spears more power. There's a kind of cup at one end, and you put the blunt end of the spear in there, and use the stick like an extension of your arm. You can send a spear for miles, with one of them! He wanted to take me hunting with him once, but Mum said no - I guess she was afraid I'd get hurt, or something. He stayed with us for a long time, but then one day, not long before Cobbo came, he told Mum he had to go. Walkabout, they call it - it's a kind of culture thing, something they have to do every so often, I think.

Any way, right from the first, Cobbo treated me differently from the way the other men did. He would always take the time to talk to me for a minute or two, if he saw me out in the yard or somewhere – and when he came to the house, as he did most evenings, he'd sit down with me and ask how my day had been, what I'd been doing for school, and tell me about his day. At first, I thought Mum would tell him not to, but she didn't say anything – and it was pretty clear that she liked him, too. When he came in, she'd pour him a mug of tea, and often sit down to talk to him at the kitchen table for a while – or if she was busy, they'd talk while she got on with whatever she was doing.

I guess, too, he was what I'd call a gentleman. To most folks, I suppose he looked like an ordinary rough-necked swaggie, and maybe sounded like one, too. But I never heard him swear in front of my mother – and with me, it would always be 'little' swear-words, like 'flaming' or 'Blimey' But he could let rip with the best of them, if he had to! I overheard him once, I remember – he was in the bunkhouse with the other men, and one of them had been complaining about something or another. I was just outside, fetching some wood for the stove, and I heard him, his voice raised in anger:

'Listen, mate! You've got life pretty f******g easy here compared with some places I've worked! Just be f*****g grateful for what you've got – Mrs Westrom lets you get away with bloody murder half the time, <u>and</u> pays you over the f*****g odds as well, so either put up or shut up! Get on with it, or bugger off somewhere else if you don't like it!'

I think that was one reason why I came to have so much respect for him – he knew exactly how to treat different people, where to draw the line. And he respected <u>me</u> – he spoke to me in a different way from the way he'd talk to the other men, and different again from the way he spoke to my Mum. He recognised that I was a different person, and that made me feel that I mattered, even if I was only a kid. People don't realise how important that is – if kids think they're being treated as second-class people, then that's what they'll be.

I never learned much about where he'd come from. He didn't seem to want to talk about it, and I guess, at first, I was too afraid to ask. By the time I'd become comfortable enough to feel I <u>could</u> ask, it didn't seem to matter much any more. I know he came from the south, Victoria or New South Wales, because he did say once that where he came from, they mostly played Aussie Rules football. Sport was one of our frequent topics of conversation – in the evenings, when he was at the house, we'd talk about whatever cricket matches were on, or about the rugby in the winter. We had a good laugh about beating England for the ashes – he could remember each series, over a lot of years, right back to the time we lost to Peter May's team. He did let slip a bit more about what he'd done before, just once – but I'll come to that later.

Like I said, he was a gentleman. He always treated my mother with respect – it was either 'Ma'am' or 'Mrs Westrom' for ages. She would ask him, every now and then, to call her Angie, but he resisted – it was quite a shock when at last, one day when the three of us were sitting at the kitchen table over mugs of tea, he did cave in. But even then, he would only use her Christian name if there was no-one else around – in front of the others, it was still 'Mrs Westrom', all the time.

I like to do my homework in the kitchen, late in the afternoon while Mum's cooking the dinner – it's nice to have her company, the bustle of her working in the background. And the supply of fresh drinks is good, too. And Cobbo took an interest in my school work. Not just pretending to – he'd ask about my day, like I said, and then if I had any homework to do. Most nights, I did, and he'd happily sit with me and look over it. He was really clever too, and educated – he might have seemed like a rough station hand to other people, but they hadn't heard him declaiming a Shakespeare sonnet, or listened to him explaining Newton's Laws of Physics. And he would always help me, if I needed it. He seemed to know all the answers – but he wouldn't just tell me what they were! Rather, he'd sit beside me at the table, and patiently lead me along until I got there myself. Essays about History or Geography, or for English, he'd just kind of nudge at me until I did it right – if there was something, some fact I'd got wrong, he'd quietly suggest that I ought to think about it, and that was enough of a clue for me to question my own work – and then, if I didn't know the answer, he'd point me in the right direction to find out, suggest which books to look in.

And maths – I was never very good at maths. But with Cobbo's help, my grades went up dramatically! But again, he wouldn't tell me any answers, just nudge and prod at me mentally until I found my own way to the right answer. Rather like, at shearing or dip time, he'd use a prod to urge a reluctant ram in the right direction. That way, I actually learnt how to solve the problems that were set – and even now, I'm much better at maths than I'd ever expected to be. Thanks to him.

I guess he taught me an awful lot. If I think about it now, I can see that he actually taught me much more than I ever realised. It's not just my school work, he changed the way I think, the way I <u>am</u>. I used to be a quiet sort of kid, a bit shy maybe, and always afraid to make decisions, to trust my own judgement. I used to rely on my Mum for all that, she would always tell me what to do. But he would let me, no, I guess <u>make</u> me take decisions, even if they were small, unimportant ones. On quiet days, he'd sometimes take me out in the bush with him – with mum's permission, of course. We'd go out, on foot or on horseback, and he'd suddenly ask: 'Which way shall we go?' And then refuse to even make a suggestion, which left me to decide. Or it would be 'Shall we go fishing today, or riding?'

And in whatever we were doing, he trusted me. Out in the bush, on a horse, fishing, shooting, his manner always said that I was his equal. He would trust me to load his rifle, saddle his horse, and later, even drive that knocked-about old Holden around the station. And because he trusted me, I learnt to trust myself. I learnt not to be afraid to make decisions:

'Life's all about decisions, Jacko-boy. You'll have no choice but to make a lot of 'em, in the years to come. The trick is to try and make the right ones, while not being afraid to make the wrong ones. I've made plenty of wrong ones, believe me! And I'm sure I'll make plenty more. But making <u>no</u> decision is always wrong, right? The good men are just the ones who made more right decisions than wrong ones.'

For sure, he has changed me a lot. He's made me the boy I am now – and I guess he's made me the man I will be, in a few years time. I hope, if he ever does come back, that he'll be proud of me, of the person he helped me to be.

The old man paused in his reading and laid the exercise book aside. He groped for another bottle and knocked the cap off, took a quick mouthful and stood it back on the bedside unit. His eyes sought the window, and the night's darkness outside; a wind had got up, moaning softly around the veranda and adding a counterpoint to his sombre thoughts as he gazed into a distance that only he could see. The sigh he gave shivered in his throat, and he picked the book up again...

Jacko-boy. That was what he always called me. Within days of his arrival, I think we both felt a kind of friendship growing between us. 'Jack' quickly became 'Jacko', and then he added the '-boy' on the end. I loved it – it made me feel all the more special, all the more important, because he thought I was worth a special name like that.

I didn't have many friends – in the outback, we're all too far apart to make real friendships! There's Johnny Miller, of course – his family own the next station, Worrongatta. Their house is about twenty miles away, and we get together pretty often. They sometimes ask Mum and me over for a meal, or they come here, which is great because Johnny and I get to play together for a bit. And we chat over the radio sometimes, when there's nothing important on the air. My other good mate is Mark Krascjyk, in the town. His Dad owns the little garage there, and we get to see each other from time to time, either when I get to go into town with Mum or whoever does the weekly run, or sometimes if his Dad comes out to the station, to fix any of the machinery or service the ute or Mum's car. Mark's about eight months younger than me, but Johnny's a year older.

But of course that's different – you can't have the same kind of friendship with a grown-up man as you can with another kid. Although there were times when Cobbo seemed almost like another kid – he'd get just as excited when he caught a big fish, or hit a six in the yard when we were playing cricket. And he'd sometimes wrestle me – I'm very ticklish, and he quickly found out about that, so it soon became a kind of game – I'd say something cheeky to him, and he'd grab me and tickle me until I squealed. Or if I managed to run off, he'd chase me – I'm pretty quick on my feet, but he was much faster than you'd imagine, and usually caught me before I'd got very far.

Very soon, he seemed more like part of the family than a hired man, especially to me. But even then, he wouldn't, himself, assume any privileges. If he thought mum was being too friendly, he'd remind us: 'I'm just one of the hands, Angie'. And once, I asked him why people called him Cobbo:

'It's after Cobb & Co – you know, the company that used to run the stagecoaches all over Australia? Years ago, someone called me that because I'm always on the move, never stay in one place too long.'

I guess that should have been a bit of a warning – but I didn't want to hear that. I wanted him to stay with us, and I think I would have deliberately ignored even the strongest of hints.

I've just read back over what I've written so far. It's pretty chaotic – my brain seems to be jumping all over the place. I nearly tore it all up and started over again, but I don't think I can. Now I have started, I kind of want to get it done and finished – the idea was to flush out the memories, take the sting out of them, but right now they feel much worse than ever. I guess I'm stirring them up, and now I'm on the way, going back to start over again is just a step too far, even if what I've said up to now is a jumbled mess! I'd better try and get my brain into order.

Memories – so many of them! A year and a half's worth. I'll try to put things in the order they happened – well, more or less.

Although we got on really well, right from the start, I still felt a kind of shyness with him to begin with. He clearly liked me, and like I said, he would take the time to talk to me, to be with me, but I wasn't entirely sure of this strange fellow who'd suddenly turned up out of the blue, and begun to treat me like I was somewhere between a friend and a son. But it didn't take me too long to get over that, as you will have gathered already! It was my Mum who started the homework thing – it was only a few weeks after he'd come, and she knew I was struggling with some maths. Algebra – despite the carefully explained lesson on the radio, it was still a complete mystery to me:

'Cobbo? You any good at algebra?' He shrugged:

'I can manage if I have to, Ma'am.'

'Would you give Jack some help? It's the one subject he's not so good at.' Not so good? I was hopeless!

'I'll give it a go.'

'Would you mind? I don't want to impose on you.'

'No worries! I'd be happy.' He came and sat down beside me at the table: 'What have yeh got there, Jacko? Let's have a gander.'

He set about coaxing and teasing at me, nudging my sense of logic along until half an hour later the list of problems were all solved, to his satisfaction and my delight. And from then on, he would always ask what homework I had, and give me help if I needed it. When I didn't, I would show him my completed work, and he would read it through with a serious expression on his face. Sometimes, he'd suggest ways of improving it, often correcting my rather dodgy English; other times, he'd just say:

'That looks fine to me, Jacko-boy!' And his congratulation was usually accompanied by a hearty slap on the back, which would make me grin even as I pretended to flinch. Before long, it was a source of real pride to hear that phrase from his lips, to have his commendation on my work, and I looked forward each evening to showing him what I'd done. When he was away for a few days, about the property, I'd keep everything together to show him when he got back.

Spring moved on – October became November, and by the end of that month the weather was getting hotter. It was too early for the rains, and the creek was getting real low. We were okay at the house – there's a small bore that feeds a big tank behind the bunkhouse, up on stilts, but it was getting too dry out there for the sheep. My Dad had set up a run-off which would divert some of the bore water into the creek, but it had fallen into disuse over a series of wet summers; Cobbo had taken a look at it:

'Mrs Westrom?' He came into the kitchen late one evening.

'Yes, Cobbo?'

'The run-off, from the house water tank – would it be okay if I tried to get it working? Only the creek's pretty low and the sheep are suffering.' She turned to him, flour on her hands from the bread she was baking:

'It's not been used for years – but I think it'll still work if we need it.'

'Reckon so, Ma'am. The pipes look okay to me, it's just the screw valve that's stuck, probably rusted up. Shall I try 'n fix it?'

'Yes, do, Cobbo.'

'Tomorrow, then.' He turned to me: 'You goin' to come and help, Jacko-boy?' I looked up from the English essay I was just finishing:

'Can I?'

'Sure you can. If your mother doesn't mind?' She laughed – it was a sound I was beginning to get used to hearing again:

'Not while the school broadcasts are on, all right?'

'All right, Mum!' Cobbo grinned down at me:

'Seven o'clock okay for you, laddie?'

'Yeah, sure!' We were usually up by then anyway, and it gave me a real thrill to be asked to help with one of his jobs.

Next morning, I was up even before time, ready and waiting for his knock at the door. It was already getting hot outside, a bright clear sun striking across the bush as we strolled around to the water-tank on its high tower. Cobbo had a bunch of tools in his big brown hands, and I carried the ladder. The run-off pipe comes out about half-way up the tank, so that even if it got left on by mistake, it wouldn't drain out all of the water, and the valve was on the side of the tank. I leant the ladder up in place, where he told me, and he climbed up it:

'Main thing I need you to do, Jacko, is to stand on the bottom rung of the ladder, right? That's so it doesn't slip – if I came down from right up there it'd hurt a bit!'

I stood there as he directed, watching as he squirted oil all over the reluctant valve and set about trying to ease it into motion with a pair of Stilsons. It took a while, and I began to get a bit bored, started looking around the yard, watching some of the dogs playing together as they wolfed down the food Mum had taken out for them. Then there was a kind of groaning noise from over my head – I looked up, thinking Cobbo had hurt himself, only to see him grinning down at me:

'It's comin', Jacko-boy!' He heaved on the wrench again, and the valve's wheel moved a little more, making that groaning noise again. Another heave, and it suddenly gave – he almost lost his balance, but grabbed the top of the ladder. I hung on, to stop it moving – and was suddenly drenched with water from above! Next thing I heard was him laughing – he stood looking down at me, just roaring with laughter:

'If you could see the look on your face, lad!' Then I was laughing too – a weak spot in the pipe had given way under the strain as he freed the valve, and now water was leaking out, directly above where I was standing. It felt cool and refreshing – I whipped off my shirt, and danced around under it for a moment, before he screwed the valve shut again:

'Mustn't waste the water, Jacko, we don't know how much of it we'll need before the rains come.'

I stayed where I was, my clothes beginning to dry in the morning sun, while he went off to the sheds to look for something to repair the pipe. Minutes later he was back, a piece of tin and several big jubilee clips in his hands. He went up the ladder again:

'On the bottom with you, Jacko. I'm goin' to have to lean pretty far out to do this, so I'm relying on you, right?' I took my place there again, leaning in against the rungs to make sure it wouldn't slip or topple back, the occasional drip still landing on my bare back. It took him a couple of minutes to get the tin around the pipe and tighten the clips on it; then he turned the valve on again, and now only a few drops of water escaped:

'Yeah – that'll do for now, Jacko-boy! I'll get a new section of pipe next time we're at the store in town and fix it properly.'

He left the valve running slowly through that morning – there was a gentle breeze turning the windmill, pumping water up from the bore. I helped him take the tools and the ladder back to the shed, and then we walked together, back to the house. My Mum stared at me when we got there:

'What have you been up to, young man?' Cobbo laughed:

'It's his own fault, Mrs Westrom. He banged his head on the pipe, and his skull's so hard he actually cracked it open.'

'I did not!' She joined in his laughter as I protested my innocence.

'There was a weak spot in the pipe' he confessed 'and it gave way when I got the valve turning. I've fixed it, for now, and I'll do it properly when I can get a new piece of pipe from the store.'

'But there's water going out for the sheep?'

'That's right, Ma'am.' She looked at me:

'You'd better go and change, Jack. Hang those wet clothes on the line, okay?'

As I went to do as she told me, it crossed my mind to wonder if Cobbo had <u>known</u> there was that weak spot in the pipe. He'd inspected it all the day before – had he put me and the ladder directly under it on purpose? I couldn't help a big grin at the idea, as I stripped off and searched in the drawer for a dry pair of pants.

A smile crossed the old man's face at the memory. He took another, longer pull from the bottle by his side, shaking his head as he put it down again and returned to the exercise book...

It was that incident with the water-tank which kind of set the seal on our friendship, I think. And yes, I think he did set it up – or at least, he put me there, knowing what might happen! It was always with me that his sense of humour would show itself – I know the other men thought of him as rather straight-laced, a bit serious, maybe, and certainly when he was working he was totally focussed on the job. He didn't take every opportunity to drive into town, to the pub, the way they did. Oh, he did enjoy a beer, for sure, but he'd make the trip to the Kananga maybe every other week, on a weekend, and then he'd pretty much let his hair down. Maybe that wasn't such a good example to me – he'd always drive himself in that old Holden, and then drive back after a fair skinful. I suppose there wasn't too much for him to run into around there – the odd kangaroo, perhaps, or one of the sheep – not that he ever did, as far as I knew anyway. And the next morning, he'd be up with the sun as usual, just as bright and cheerful as ever.

Cobbo had a liking for VB, Victoria Bitter – another indication that he'd come from down that way, I guess – but you couldn't get it easily around our way. But Mum had a word with the bottle shop in town; they'd get her a couple of cases every now and again, and she'd keep them in the fridge for him. We've got a second fridge, out under the back veranda, where Mum always keeps a few bottles of cold water and even some orange or lemon squash, diluted ready to drink, for me. Out here in the bush, we haven't got any electricity – not yet, anyway. They've got it in town, and Mum and Mr Miller have been talking about sharing the cost of having a line put in which would come to us and then go on to Worrongatta. We've got a generator – I've said that before, haven't I? – which powers the equipment around the station, but we don't use it for the house. We charge batteries from it, which is what runs the wireless, and the two-way radio. If the batteries run down in the middle of something, like one of my lessons, I have to pedal the old cranked genny to keep it going! That's happened a few times, I can tell you – now, I always make sure the batteries are charged right up before I start.

We've got kerosene lamps for light in the evenings – they're not that good, but we manage. Mum doesn't like me reading with them, she says it's bad for my eyesight, so I try to read during daylight. I've got a lamp right by my bed, real close, and I read when I go to bed most nights, but not for too long. Mum uses the old wood-burner range for most of the cooking, but she's got a smaller kero-fired one as a stand-by, which she prefers sometimes if she's only doing something quick. The fridges are run on kerosene too, so we get through quite a bit of that – we get it from the store in town – someone goes in every week, to refill the empties and get diesel for the generator as well as buying provisions and things. Mum still uses the old Coolgardie Safe which stands outside the kitchen, in its shade, to keep a lot of things like the meat and milk for the day's use cold and fresh. They're a clever kind of thing – the outside is all made of sacking, with a tray at the top which you fill with water. The water percolates through the sacking and gets evaporated by the breeze, and that keeps everything pretty cold, especially if the sun can't get on it. Doesn't use any kero or electric!

First time Mum got Cobbo some VB, she hadn't told him – he came over that evening, and she asked him, all innocently, if he'd like a cold drink:

'Sure would, Ma'am.'

'There's some in the fridge, outside – help yourself.'

He opened the fridge door:

'Oh, hey! Fair dinkum! You got those for me?'

'Of course – they're hardly for Jack!'

'Oh, well – you shouldn'a, Mrs Westrom. It's real nice of you.'

'Are you going to open one, then?'

'Right-o!' He gave me a big grin as he took one and twisted the cap off, inclined his head to me as he took a long swig from it. I grinned back – he knew the information had come from me, because we'd been talking a bit before; somehow we'd got onto drinks and he'd said about liking VB: 'But yeh can't get it around these parts, Jacko. More's the pity!'

The old man laid the book in his lap, that sad smile on his face again, and glanced at the bottle beside him: *Yeh can get it anywhere across Australia nowadays!* He took another quick swig and picked Jack's story up, went on reading...

The wet started a few weeks after we'd fixed the run-off. Clouds began to build along the horizon, and creep towards us the way they always did; a few light drops, and then it started in earnest. Every day we got a good drenching, maybe two, and in no time the bush around us was all green and glorious. It doesn't matter how often it happens – I've seen it every year of my life, after all – but it never fails to amaze me how the dry red ground can so suddenly be entirely hidden beneath a layer of bright green as the Mitchell Grass and Sorghum spring into life again.

I've always loved the wet. When I was a little kid, Mum used to send me out into a heavy downpour with a bar of soap and a flannel:

'Go on Jack – time for a free shower!' Then I'd run back into the house, where she'd grab me and towel me down as I giggled my head off. Great times. I don't do that now – I'm thirteen, after all, a bit old to run around naked in front of anyone, even my Mum. Even at eleven, I'd given away the free showers – but I still would love to go out of doors in the rain, shirtless of course, and just stand there while it soaked my hair and streamed down my skin. One of the hands we've got working here now is an English guy, Wayne Grimble, and he laughed the first time he saw me do that:

'You wouldn't do that where I come from!' He says they get most of the rain there in the winter, and it's real cold then, much colder even than our winters. He's okay, he talks to me now and then about England, and I guess I quite like him – but he's not Cobbo, you know? I think I'd quite like to go there one day – I'd like to see snow, one day! And play snowballs. But I don't think I'd want to stay too long, if it gets that cold. Grim says that even in their summer, it's about as warm as it is here in the winter – can you imagine that? He told me once that one winter, when he still lived there, it froze up on Boxing Day – their winter's the other end of the year from ours – Christmas in the snow and ice! – and didn't thaw until three months later. Makes you wonder how anyone can live through it.

Like I said, the wet's a pretty special time for me. It's when the station seems to come alive and even the sheep seem to like it – I guess they get to eat well for a while, and I suppose they enjoy that. Can sheep enjoy things, do their brains work like that? I don't really know. It's why we lamb in the early spring, because that way there's plenty of fresh green grass for them to feed on as they grow up. And then, when the lambs are older, we shear at the beginning of the summer, so the sheep don't have to carry all that wool through the hottest weather. Anyway, when it rains, everyone goes round with big smiles for a while, and it's great to have more water than we need. Most of the time we have to be pretty careful how we use water, but in the wet we can afford to waste it.

I said just now that I don't go for the free showers any more — but I still skinny-dip in the duckpond! But that's different, somehow, although if I think about, I can't see why. We call it the duckpond, but we haven't got any ducks, of course — I don't know how it came to be there, even. It's a big hollow in the ground, right next to where the creek always overflows, and it holds water for ages — Cobbo reckoned there must be a layer of clay in the bottom of it. It's great, 'cause it gives me somewhere to play, until it finally does dry up, and in the evenings it brings all kinds of wildlife to where we can see it from the house — wallabies mostly, even big reds sometimes, and dingoes. I know they're pests, but they are handsome things, even so, and I like to see them.

That first year Cobbo was here, I was splashing around, and then surfaced to find him in there with me. I was horrified for a moment, until I realised he'd still got his pants on; he laughed and asked if I minded him being there. I shook my head, and he laughed again, cupping his hands and splashing me with water. It didn't seem to matter, letting _him_ see me like that, somehow. And we were in there every evening, while it lasted, except when he was out on the station, of course. It seemed so right, the two of us laughing together like that – he'd pick me up in his strong hands and upend me into the water, and I'd come to the surface, choking and laughing, and he'd do it again.

I only went in the duckpond once this summer. It felt so lonely that I didn't want to do it again, even when Johnny came over for the day.

The old man raised his eyes from the notebook and closed them against the sting of tears. He drew breath and let out a long, shivering sigh: *Oh Jacko...* He took a long draft from the bottle at his side, and looked down again at the scribbled text...

After the run-off valve, Cobbo began to take me along when he did odd jobs around the homestead. His head would appear around the door:

'Hey, Jacko-boy – I'm goin' to fix that stable-door (or the overhead cables, or the paddock fence, or whatever) are you comin' to help?' And I'd go, of course. Even if I couldn't actually do anything to help, I'd sit close by and we'd talk, about anything and nothing, I guess. He'd always tell me what he was doing, explain not just how, but why, so that I'd understand why it mattered. And as time passed, he'd take me out into the station with him if he was off to do a quick job somewhere, so that he'd be back before dinner in the evening. My Mum wasn't too keen on this, sometimes, she thought it'd get in the way of my school work – but then she'd record any lessons off the radio so that I could catch up later. And Cobbo would make sure I did, too – if I was reluctant, he'd keep on at me until I did. And they were right, of course – even if I'm going to run the Kananga when I'm grown up, I need a decent education – farming's going to get even more technical in the future, and I'll need to be able to understand it all, and deal with the finances and the paperwork.

It was on one of those outback expeditions that he got the scar on his cheek. That was the only time he ever swore in front of me, too. We were out, a few miles from home, in his old ute, where a length of fence needed replacing. We were using a post and wire fence – the posts were still pretty much okay, but a lot of the wire had snapped or got pushed so that it fell loose, and it was easier, as Cobbo explained, to simply replace the wires over that section. We'd done most of it – he'd attached another length of the heavy steel wire at one end, along the top line of the fence, and he was using the jack to put the tension into it, when it let go. There must have been a fault in the wire itself, because it just snapped, about five yards from where we were standing. I ducked, and saw him turn his back out of the corner of my eye as I did:

'Ah, shit! Jack! Are you all right, boy?' I straightened up and looked around:

'Yeah. I'm fine, it missed me.' But it hadn't missed him – he was standing with one hand clamped to his face, blood running from between his fingers. I was terrified – I thought it'd taken his eye out, but as he carefully lowered his hand I saw it was still there. The broken end of the wire had caught his cheek as it whipped back, and laid it open along his cheekbone for a couple of inches.

'Bloody Hell! How's it look, lad?' He took his hand away for me to examine the wound, although I felt his eyes running over me as he did so, making sure I really wasn't hurt. I screwed up my courage – I've never much liked the sight of blood – and went up to him. The cut was pretty deep, but it didn't look too bad, just bleeding profusely.

'I'm goin' to need your help with this, Jacko – are you okay with that?' I nodded warily:

'Yeah – I guess so.'

'Okay then. Get the water bottle, and run some water over it, right?'

'Right-o.' He always carried water in a canvas sack hitched to the bull-bar on the front of his ute where the breeze would keep it cool, and I ran and got it. He held his head tipped right back:

'Go on, Jack!' I poured the clean cold water into the wound while he held it open. I could see the pain in his eyes, but he smiled at me:

'That's fine, Jacko-boy. Now, get the medi kit, will yeh?' I searched it out of his pack and brought it over to him. He was holding the edges of the cut together now:

'How've I got it, does it look about right?'

'Yeah, pretty good' I told him.

'Right then – get a wad of the cotton, right? Fold it into a pad, big enough to cover it all, and guide me so I can hold it in the right place, okay?' I did as I was told – he took it in one hand, still holding the wound closed with the other, and let me guide his hand until he had it covering the cut completely:

'Good-o, Jack. Now, use strips of the plaster to tape it in place, right?' I cut strips from the roll of plaster and did as he said, sticking them around the edges of the cotton, careful to leave his eye clear. Blood was already beginning to stain the cotton by the time I'd finished, but he gave me another smile:

'Good job, lad, thank you. Now, let's get back to the house – and I guess I'd better try not to laugh, eh, in case I disturb your good work!' He reached into his shorts pocket and threw me the keys; I looked at him, astonished:

'Be Better if you drive, okay?' I just stared at him: 'You can drive a car, can you?'

'Er – kinda...' I knew how to drive, what to do, from watching him or the other men, but I'd never actually driven anything before. He laughed:

'Just do what I tell you, okay?'

I got nervously into the driving seat, and he got in next to me:

'You know how to start it up?' I put the key into the switch in the dash, as I'd seen him do many times – it took me a couple of tries to get it the right way up, but then I turned it to the right, again copying what I'd seen him do:

'First click turns everything on, Jacko. Now turn it again, but let it spring back when the engine's running.' The starter whirred, and I let go in panic, afraid I'd break something.

'No, you have to keep it turning long enough to get the engine goin'.' His voice was still quiet and patient; I tried again, and this time got it right.

'Good. Now, push the clutch down – that's the pedal on the left, okay? With your left foot. And then put the lever into first gear, that's towards you and down, right?' Sitting back in the seat, I couldn't reach – I had to wriggle my bottom forward and perch right on the edge. I depressed the pedal, took the end of the gearlever on the side of the steering column in my hand and moved it up towards me, then round and down. I felt it clunk in to gear, and Cobbo chuckled as a little smile spread over my face:

'You're doin' fine, Jacko-boy! Now, the middle pedal's the brakes, right? The other one, on the right, is the throttle, you push that to make the engine run faster. Give it a push, go on!' I did, and heard the engine pick up speed: 'Now, you need a few revs to get goin', right? Hold the throttle a little way down, and gently let the clutch come up.' I did, and to my amazement the old car lurched forward. But the engine had stalled. Cobbo was still as patient as ever:

'No worries, boy, just start it up again. No, take it out of gear again first.' I did as he said, and the engine sprang into life again. I put it back into first gear:

'Now – be a bit more gentle as you let the clutch in, okay?' I opened the throttle a bit, and let the other pedal rise slowly under my foot – and we were going, bumping slowly over the rough ground. Cobbo clapped me on the shoulder:

'That's great, Jacko! Take us home, boy.' I laughed, and turned the car in the direction of the house. We picked up speed as my nerves subsided under the sheer joy of what I was doing:

'You can change up now – let your foot off the throttle, push the clutch down again, and move the lever up out of first – that's right – now up again, and you'll feel it go into second. Now up with the clutch – brilliant!' It wasn't that good, really, very jerky, and I nearly stalled the engine when I didn't open the throttle again quickly enough – but we were still going. I got it up into top gear as well, and we bounced along the dusty track the few miles back home. Despite the circumstances, and my worries about what had happened to Cobbo, I found myself thoroughly enjoying the journey. I was stretching to reach the pedals, peering over the steering wheel; but I was in a boyish heaven, driving that battered old ute along a dry track in the middle of nowhere.

It was far too soon for me when the house loomed into sight – but it was a relief, too, because I knew my Mum could take a look at the gash in Cobbo's cheek. Like any station woman, she's a pretty good nurse – I guess they have to be, to cope with things like that when they happen. I blotted my copybook, though, stalling the engine again as I braked the ute to a halt by the back door; but Cobbo just laughed:

'I'll give you a few more lessons, okay, Jacko-boy? We'll have you driving at Bathurst in no time!'

My Mum came hurrying out to meet us – I guess she knew something was wrong because we were home too soon:

'What is it, Cobbo, what's happened?'

'It's okay, Angie, Jack's fine. I've just got a little cut in my cheek.' She gave me a quick look and then went to him, taking his head gently in her hands and turning it to see:

'What happened?' She was holding his jaw, so I answered:

'Wire broke, Mum. It caught him as it whipped 'round.' The cotton was pretty well soaked in blood now:

'Inside, both of you! Did you patch it up yourself?' He shook his head:

'Jacko did most of it, he was just great.'

'I only did what you told me.' I didn't want to take any credit that wasn't due.

'And you drove that truck back here?'

'Yes, Mum.' I hung my head, afraid that I was in trouble for that. She sat Cobbo down at the kitchen table; and then turned to me and gave me a quick hug:

'Good boy, I'm so proud of you. Now go and get the medicine box off the shelf for me.'

She had peeled off the old bandage by the time I put the box down on the table next to her. She examined the wound carefully – the bleeding had slowed right down by now, but it was still oozing a bit:

'It looks pretty good, Cobbo, very clean. You washed it out?'

'Yes, Ma'am. Jack did that, with water from the bottle.' She just nodded, and then set about redressing it, making a much neater job of it than I had. She stood back to admire her handiwork:

'I reckon that'll do for now. You'd better get into town and have a word with the nurse there though, just to be sure.'

'Oh, no, Angie, it'll be just fine, it's only a little graze.' He stood up and turned to me – he held his hand out: 'Thank you, Jack, you did a fine job out there.' I took his hand, slightly bemused, as he went on: 'You kept your head and did what was needed – a lot of kids couldn't have done that. I'm really proud of you.' He shook my hand with a broad smile, and I felt the pride and pleasure swell in me at his words.

'That goes for me too, Jack. You're a fine boy.' Mum took me in a hug again as he let go of my hand, and I thought I could never be so happy. But there was still one doubt in my mind:

'You didn't mind – about me driving his truck?' She shook her head, laughing:

'No! It's something I guess you'll need to learn anyhow.'

'I'll teach him properly, if that's all right?' Cobbo asked. She held me at arm's length and gazed into my eyes:

'Please, Cobbo, please do. I know he'll learn right if you teach him.'

'Thanks, Mum!' I flung my arms around her as she laughed again – now I truly was as happy as I thought it was possible to be.

Looking back now, I suppose my Mum had always been very protective towards me. I guess you can understand, after my Dad was killed – but it did seem a bit restrictive at the time. I knew that Johnny was allowed to do much more around their property, but then he's a year older than me anyway. But once Cobbo was around, she seemed to kind of let go a lot more – she seemed to be happy if I was doing things with him, letting him teach me things. She trusted him with me, and that kind of rubbed off into her trusting me more, too.

And you repaid that trust, time and again, Jacko-boy! The man drained his stubbie, reached for the other and knocked the cap off, set it at hand on the cabinet beside the bed. He drew a breath and let it out in a long sigh, and returned to the past...

That all happened a few weeks before Christmas, just as we were getting set up for shearing. We work that in with the Millers, on Worrongatta, so that the shearing gang just move on from us to them – we go first, because they've got a bigger property and it takes them longer to get all the flocks mustered. We work together, mind – their men come to help us, and our fellas go on to help them when we're all done.

Even on Kananga, it takes a while to get all the sheep in. The farthest boundary's around nine miles from the house, so you can ride out there in half a day, easy – but it takes a bit longer to bring a mob of sheep back with you! The men are usually out for a couple of nights, then they go off again for the next lot. Mum had never let me go with them – I guess she was scared to, after Dad's accident – but that year, I asked her if I could go, this time. Previous years, I'd helped out around the station, feeding the animals into the stands for shearing and running them out again afterwards, but I really wanted to go out on the muster – I'm not a great horseman, but even so I knew I could be useful. And it was experience I'll need in the end, if I'm going to take the place over one day.

She didn't want me to, but then Cobbo put his spoke in for me. And like I said just now, she'd trust him to look after me, so in the end she said okay. We set off the next morning, right out to the far side of the property where we knew one of the big flocks was gathered. We found them okay, and then set up camp for the night. What a brilliant experience! Supper of salt beef and beans, cooked over a camp-fire, a yarn by the fire afterwards with a few tinnies (Cobbo slipped me one as well – I hope Mum never sees this!), and then to bed under the stars. I rolled out my swag (a sleeping-bag and roll-up mattress – not exactly the old bushman's swag, I suppose, but it didn't matter to me!) and crawled in.

I lay there for ages, just gazing up at the wild expanse of the sky. There was no moon, just stars, millions of them, the whole sky just glittering with them. The night sky's pretty spectacular even at the house, but out there, with no other light anywhere around, it's just breath-taking. Cobbo was stretched out next to me; I felt his hand on my shoulder:

'You ever seen the like of that before, Jacko?'

'Never!' I breathed. He chuckled softly:

'Nor will you, boy, anywhere else in the world. Australia has the biggest sky you'll find anywhere.' I didn't disbelieve him. I've said somewhere, I think, that I'd always fought shy of asking Cobbo about his past, the things he'd done before – but that one time, it felt kind of right:

'Have you been to other places and seen what they're like?' I asked. For a long time, he didn't reply, and I thought he wasn't going to, but at last he said:

'Yeah. I've been a few places, Jacko-boy. Ran away from school when I was fourteen and went for a sailor. Merchant ships – I was on the P&O for ten years. I've seen most of Asia, bits of Europe. Even been to the old country, once. They're good, in their own way, I guess – but trust me, boy, there's nowhere like Australia. Nowhere you can lie back and see a sky like that one.'

The silence then seemed too precious to break. Before long, I was asleep.

Two days later we got the mob back to the station, corralled them in one of the sheds, and set off for some more. Then the shearing gang were there, settling in to the extra bunkhouse, getting set up in the sheds – and then it was all hell let loose, men working and the old generator running day and night, the rattle of the shears and the yelling of the shearers...

And then it was over, for another year. The gang moved on to Worrongatta, the sheep were dispersed again out into the bush, the trucks came and hauled the wool away, and life returned to normal.

Christmases were a pretty big occasion for us, like I guess they are for everyone – we never went mad on presents for each other, I suppose Mum and I were okay for money, but we didn't exactly throw it around. I'd get her something like perfume or some special soaps, and she'd get the latest thing in model cars for me, and maybe a board game that we could play together in the evenings. But Christmas Day was always really special.

Mum would cook up a dinner for us, and any of the hands who were staying over. Some of them would take advantage of a few days break to go and see their families, but there were usually three or four of us for Christmas dinner, and she'd really go for it – Turkey, stuffing, roast potatoes, all the trimmings. We'd eat quite late, after the heat of the day had passed – a blow-out like that would have been just too much, otherwise! And then we'd sit and talk, with a glass of wine for Mum, a few beers for the men, and a Pepsi-Cola or two for me. I'd usually get a sip or two of her wine, and a quick swig of beer when she wasn't looking!

That year, Cobbo stayed with us. But it was the week before when he really blew my mind. I've already said that by then, he and I would talk quite a lot, about all kinds of things – one day, it was one of the evenings while we were out in the bush mustering the sheep, sitting by the campfire after supper, and he was asking about the things I knew how to do, and what I didn't. He knew by that time that I could ride a horse, even if I wasn't any kind of expert – I'm still pretty ungainly in the saddle, I guess – and he'd already promised to teach me to drive properly. I remember he asked, among other things:

'Can you shoot a gun, Jacko?'

'Kinda, I guess.' That was my usual, non-committal response then to any question where I felt my skills were pretty inadequate. Cobbo knew me well enough by then to understand that, too, and he chuckled:

'Well, okay, I guess that's something else I can teach you sometime, eh?'

'Yeah, sure!' And that was it – we went on to something else, I can't remember what now.

It was the week before Christmas, the Friday, which was the day someone would go into town for supplies and the like. It was the day that the County Library came to town, and that was pretty important to me – I've already told you that I like to read, and each week I'd send back any books I had and get some new ones. I liked to go and pick my own, but mostly Mum wouldn't let me – it was usually a whole day's expedition, and she didn't like me to miss the radio lessons. She'd get some for me, if she went in, or whoever did go would try their best to get something to interest me, and usually they did pretty well. Sometimes Mum would get books I'd already read, and I'd pull her leg about her awful memory – but I'd pick them up and read them again, generally. I'm like that – I can read the same book two or three times, and get something new from it each time. Not always, of course – some books just get boring the second time around, and aren't worth bothering with.

I don't watch television – mainly because we haven't got one! But I don't think I'd watch it much if we did – I've seen it often enough, at the Miller's, and other places, and while I guess it's a bit of a novelty, it really doesn't do that much for me. Most of the programmes seem to be American stuff, and they get boring too after a bit. I like the radio, I listen to things like plays and stories – but we have to be careful because of running the batteries down – and like I say, I read a lot. I've got quite a big collection of my own books, as well as the library ones – even some poetry. Maybe that sounds a bit cissy, but what the heck? No-one's likely to read this! My favourite poetry is by a guy called Spike Milligan, and it's not like what you'd think poetry is at all! It's complete nonsense – but it's just hilarious! The guy's got to be either a genius, or totally crazy. Or maybe both.

Anyway, that Friday, Cobbo volunteered to do the run into town. At first Mum said she'd go herself, because of getting things for Christmas, but he was unusually insistent, and in the end she gave in. She wrote him a list of the things she needed him to get, and jobs to do there, and then he asked:

'Is it okay if Jack comes along?'

'Oh, I don't know, Cobbo, he'll miss his lessons again.'

'You can record them, Mum! I'll catch up later, I promise!'

'I'll make sure he does, too, Angie.'

'Oh – all right then! But no shirking your work, young man!'

'No, 'course not Mum.' I'd done my morning chores, and I knew that Cobbo would help me later if I got behind.

We drove in, in his old ute – there's a much newer one that belongs to the station, but he always preferred to use his own. He filled its tank at the garage, got the kerosene cans all refilled and got a few cans of diesel for the generator, while Mark and I got together for a good old yarn. I wanted to stay with Mark while he did the other errands, but he insisted that I went with him into the store.

He went through Mum's list of groceries, and added a case of Pepsi-Cola with a wink at me – he knew it was my favourite, although Mum didn't like me to have too much of it – she thinks sugary drinks like that aren't good for my teeth, and I suppose she's right. He paid for the turkey she'd already ordered, told the storeman that we'd be in to get it on Christmas Eve.

Then he said to the man:

'Do you carry air-guns?' It's the kind of store that sells pretty well anything and everything, like most of them in the outback I reckon, and the man said yes they did.

'Can I have a look at one? A rifle – something decent, none of the cheap rubbish that's about these days.' The storeman grinned and turned to pick a long narrow box off of a high shelf behind him:

'Try this, mate.' Cobbo opened the box and lifted the gun out. He turned it over in his hands, a critical look on his face:

'I guess it'd do, but it ain't what we're lookin' for. What d'yeh reckon, Jacko?' He handed it to me, and I looked at him, surprised. 'Well?'

'Looks okay to me' I said.

'Ye-ah... But look here – the finish on the metal 'round the action's a bit iffy with those rough edges. And the stock's Bakelite, there – I don't like that too much.' He worked the gun: 'And the action's a bit stiff. What's the price?' he asked the storeman. The man gave him a figure: 'Yeh got anythin' better?'

'Yeah, if yeh don't mind payin' for it – hold on a minute, it's in the back room.' The storeman left us, and I asked:

'What do you want it for, Cobbo?'

'Tell yeh later, Jacko-boy. You think that one looks okay?' I shrugged – he obviously didn't. 'Listen, Jack – a weapon is like a tool, okay? It _is_ a tool, for a grazier like you, or a station hand like me.

And weapons, like any other tool, you get what you pay for, right? It's worth paying what you can afford, to get the best you can, because that way it'll last you a lifetime. Cheap crap'll let you down when you most need it. Remember that, boy.'

I just nodded; moments later, the storeman was back:

'How 'bout this? It's the one most men seem to get on with – it's well made, a real quality job, and dead accurate, if you know what you're doing with it. It'll flatten a rat right across the yard – that's what most folk want, I guess?' He held the gun out to Cobbo, and I'm sure my jaw dropped. The rifle in his hands was the most striking thing I'd seen – clean and purposeful, its metal with that evil blue-black sheen that seems so right on a lethal weapon, its wooden stock polished to a warm golden shine. Cobbo was grinning:

'That's more like it! This looks pretty good to me. Aussie made?' The man laughed:

'Nah – British! One thing the Poms can do is make a decent gun, and this is as good as they get, mate. That there's real English oak' he indicated the stock.

'Right-o. How much?' The man quoted a price that made me flinch, and Cobbo pursed his own lips. The store owner gave a despairing sigh:

'All right mate – I reckon I can do you a bit off of that, if you want it.' Still Cobbo hesitated, but then he said:

'Yeah – okay, we'll take it. But that's on my personal tab, right, not the Station's.'

'Sure thing, mate.'

'And I'd better have a coupl'a boxes of pellets for it.'

'Sure – three for the price o' two, how's that?'

'Good on yeh!'

Cobbo signed the tabs, and I helped him to carry the boxes of kit and provisions out to the ute. We went back then, for the last things – he took the rifle from the counter, and handed it to me:

'You'd better carry that, Jacko.' I felt kind of privileged to even have my hands on it, and asked him why; he chuckled:

''Cause it's yours, boy.' I know my jaw fell open this time. I stood staring from him to the gun in my hands:

'Mine?'

'Yours, Jacko-boy. Your Christmas present, from me, okay?'

'But... But...' All I could do was stutter like an idiot, and he laughed:

'Come on, boy, into the truck with you, unless you're going to stand there all day?'

He picked up the last of the boxes, and I followed him out to the ute. I must have still been looking stunned, because he looked at me as he got into the driving seat and laughed:

'Is that okay for yeh, Jacko-boy?' I struggled to say anything:

'Yeah – oh, yeah! It's...' All I could do was shake my head in wonder, and he laughed again:

'Listen – if I want to spend my cash on a grubby kid like you, that's my affair, right?' Now, I grinned at him in delight:

'Right...' He reached out and took my shoulder in his hand, a serious look suddenly on his face:

'Listen to me, Jack. I've spoken to your Mum about this, and at first she wasn't too keen. She thinks you're too young for it, but I talked her 'round – she knows you'll need to know how to use a gun properly one day, and I think she trusts me to teach you. And I convinced her that even though you're only eleven, you're not a stupid kid. We both know you've got the brains to learn what you need to know, and the wit to be sensible with it, right? A lot of airguns are no more than toys – but what you've got there is anything but, you understand? That's a real weapon, and it can kill you as easily as it can kill rats or dingoes. You have to accept that there are rules, okay?'

'Yeah, of course...' My mind was still in a whirl. He went on:

'No-one but me teaches you to use it, okay? I don't want you listening to any half-baked ideas from anyone else about what you can and can't do. And you don't even touch it, get it from the rack, unless I'm there with you.'

I just nodded, my eyes fixed on the beautiful rifle in my hands. Cobbo was still talking:

'You never, never, never, fool around with it, or let your mates play with it. And remember this – a man never points a gun at anything he doesn't want to shoot, right?'

'Right, Cobbo.' I looked up at him, and felt tears rising to my eyes: 'Thank you – thank you...' He clapped me on the shoulder:

'No worries, kid! Just show me you can be responsible about the way you use it and look after it, okay?'

'Okay!'

Christmas Day was the usual joyful occasion. I think everyone enjoyed themselves – I know I did! And over the weeks that followed, Cobbo was as good as his word. He taught me how to use the rifle, not just shooting with it, but how to look after it, how to dismantle it and clean it. And he insisted that I always did that, every time I got it out, no matter how much or how little it had been used:

'Always put your gun away clean, Jacko, that way it's always ready to be used when you need it – and you never know how quickly you might need it, one day.'

I was an eager student, too. Every time we got that gun out, I felt a kind of rush of disbelief that it really was mine, that such a beautiful thing belonged to me. And I treated it with the respect it deserved – however beautiful it might be, there was still something evil about it. I guess it was because I knew it could kill me, or anyone around me – and because of the way Cobbo himself always treated it, and indeed any gun, with the utmost respect. And I got to be pretty good with it, too. I could soon pot an empty can off of a fence-post all the way across our yard; and then Cobbo would throw the cans for me, rolling them along the ground, so I could get some practice at hitting moving targets. And I got to be fair dinkum at that, too, in time.

He set about teaching me to drive, like he'd promised, as well. He put an old pillow on the seat of his ancient Holden, behind my back, to bring me closer to the wheel and the pedals, and we'd bump and bounce around the yard for hours at a time until he was happy that I could really control it. Then he'd take me out into the bush, to a clear area where I could get some speed up. That was really exhilarating – even at thirty miles an hour, to a kid like me it felt like I was breaking the land speed record, like that Campbell guy from England had done at Lake Eyre a few years ago.

After a while, he let me drive it on the roads close to the Station. I don't know if that was really legal – probably not! But Cobbo never seemed to care too much about things like that – and he always seemed to get away with it, too. But I seem to be getting ahead of myself!

I said before that I never got to know much about Cobbo, who he was or where he came from, but I suppose, now that I'm thinking about it, I knew more about him than I realised. It just seemed to come out in little bits, so it never seemed to add up to anything. It was on

Christmas Day, after dinner in the evening, when Mum asked him about himself. I guess she was as curious as me, but like me hadn't liked to ask before. But then, we'd had some drinks – Cobbo'd had a good few beers, and Mum was at least halfway down a bottle of wine. I reckon I'd had the best part of can of beer, in odd 'tastes' from everyone else, and I remember I was feeling a bit cross-eyed too. Anyway, in a lull in the conversation, she suddenly turned to him and asked:

'Who _are_ you, Cobbo? Where'd you come from?' He looked at her, but he didn't reply at first. I didn't think he was going to, but then he just shrugged and said:

'Oh, here 'n there. Everywhere and nowhere!' But Mum wasn't taking that for an answer:

'Come on, Cobbo – were you born here in Australia?' Again, he took his time replying, and I got the feeling he didn't want to. But maybe he felt he owed her something, since she'd asked:

'Yes.' He hesitated, but then he went on: 'My folks came here in the thirties, just before the war. My father walked out on his family – or maybe they practically threw him out. They didn't like his choice of bride – it just wasn't done, not in England anyway, for the son of the family to marry the kitchen-maid. He joined the Anzac forces at the start of the war, and he never came back. He died on the Kokoda track.'

There was a kind of collective in-drawing of breath around the table – even I know the stories of the massacre that had happened there. Mum put her hand on his arm in sympathy, but he smiled:

'It was a long time ago.'

'What about you, Cobbo?' I think she asked it to change the subject, to move it on. Again, he didn't answer straight away, but then he just said:

'I've made my own way in the world since I was fourteen. Australia lets you do that.'

I remembered then what he'd said to me, that night under the stars, about having been a sailor for ten years, and I thought that I'd like to know more about it. I opened my mouth to ask him, but he looked at me, and I saw something in his eyes – not a warning look, exactly, but I knew he didn't want to talk about himself any more. So I shut up, and took a swig from my bottle of Pepsi instead.

The old man laid the book aside, got up from the bed and stretched his back. He walked over to the window and cracked it open; outside, the breeze had brought clouds overhead, and a gentle rain was falling. Looking up, he watched as the moon escaped for a moment through a break in the clouds, and then was swallowed up once more. He sighed, and rubbed his face with his hands, looked around at the old exercise book lying on the bed. A rueful smile crossed his lined face, and he went to lie down again, the fresh smell of the rain pervading the room...

A couple of weeks after Christmas, the Millers came over for dinner on the Sunday, and I got to show Johnny my gun. We'd been to them for Boxing Day, and I'd taken my other presents then so that we could compare results, but, mindful of Cobbo's warning, I hadn't dared take the rifle along. When he saw it, Johnny was gobsmacked:

'Hey! That trumps everything I got in one go!' His folks were rather better off than us, and he usually did better than me, come Christmas and birthdays. But he wasn't jealous – he's a great friend to have. He was a bit funny when I said I wouldn't take it out of the cabinet for him – His Dad lets him take his own gun out whenever he wants, for practice, but I wouldn't go against Cobbo's orders. But when Cobbo came home later that day, we took it out in the yard so I could show off my prowess, such as it was then! He let Johnny have a go, too, and he was really impressed with it. We took turns potting empty beer cans off the fence posts – Johnny did better than me, but then he'd had a lot more practice, and he whistled:

'This is a beaut, Jack! It's better than my gun, as good as my Dad's, I reckon – swap yeh?' His offer was made in jest, and I just laughed:

'Get out of here!'

That summer dragged on – all through the hottest time, I didn't see so much of Cobbo, because he and the other men would be up and out before first light so they could get the work started before the heat of the day, and then rest through the worst of it before working on in the evenings. If they were close by, they'd come back for a bite of lunch, but mostly they'd be out all day until after dark. Sometimes he'd come to the house and sit with me for a while – homework again! – and talk to mum. He'd stop by to report what they'd done for her, of course, pretty well every day, but often he'd be so tired he wouldn't hang around.

I guess I've given you the impression that my life is just school work or enjoying myself. That's not really true, of course – I've got my chores to do every day, mostly to help Mum. I help her with jobs like cleaning the house, sweeping and dusting – she hates it if home starts looking scruffy – and I look after and feed the dogs, most days, and the chickens. Fresh eggs everyday for breakfast! And we keep a couple of cows, for the milk – Cobbo used to pull my leg about being a real hot-shot milkmaid. One of the men, Abraham, is brilliant with horses – he's a half-caste abo, a real nice fellow but very shy, and he's worked with horses all his life, I guess. I often help him, as well, around the stables. So it's not like I have time to get bored, or anything.

But eventually autumn arrived, and Cobbo would be around a lot more, especially in the evenings after he'd finished work for the day. That was when he really got into teaching me to shoot, and to drive. After a couple of months of his teaching, and a lot of practice, I could hit pretty well anything he told me to – we'd take a turn around the yard and the sheds, looking for rats, and I'd get most of them first time. I was so proud of myself! Even Mum looked pleased – I guess she'd got over her reluctance for me to have the gun, probably because Cobbo had kept me in line with it, and instilled in me his own wariness of such weapons.

And by the time Easter was approaching, whenever Mum let me go into town with him, I'd drive most of the way. He wouldn't let me actually drive right into town – he said we could both get into trouble if anyone reported us. We'd pass an occasional car or truck on the highway, and get a kind of startled look when they saw a kid of eleven at the wheel, but no-one ever dropped us in it with the local constable. Not that Constable MacManus would have done anything except tell us not get caught again, I suspect! He'd a real good guy, keeps order around here without being nasty or officious about it.

It was that autumn, about the time the rains dried up, that I broke my ankle. The creek was still running well – we'd had quite a wet summer, even if it had been a bit late starting – and the duckpond was still full, I remember. Talking about that – I asked Cobbo how he thought it had come to be there, and he reckoned it was man-made:

'It's too regular in shape, and too darned convenient, to be there by chance, Jacko. I reckon some owner of the station, mebbe a long time ago, dug it out and brought in clay to line it. Long before they put the bore down, I'd guess. That way it'd be like a reservoir – the rains would fill it up, when the creek ran over – that'll be why the bank between them is kinda low, see? And we know it holds water for quite a while, until the sun dries it up. And the trees that shade it – they'll have put them in too, to keep the sun off and make it last as long as possible, right? Now we've got the bore, it doesn't serve much purpose any more. Except for you to try and drown yourself in, of course!'

The trees are a couple of rows of tired-looking old ghost gums. Like the rest of the vegetation, they spring into life in the rains, and then they throw shadows over the pond for much of the hottest part of the day. There's some more that shade the house, the same way – but they're more like a natural thicket. I suppose they'd built the house where it is because of the trees, to make use of their shade. They'd always been there, at least as far as I knew, so I'd never given them any thought – that was something else I guess Cobbo gave me – the ability to really look at things around me, and think about them. When you do look, and think, it's pretty obvious that those trees around the pond didn't get there by accident.

When I was very small, my Dad had put up a rope swing on a big branch, right by the side of the pond. After he died, I didn't use it for ages, but then one day when I was about six or seven, one of the men we had there then fixed it up, and shortened the ropes so it would fit me again, and I began to play on it from time to time. And as I grew taller, I would knot the ropes to shorten them again and again. Maybe it sounds a bit cissy for a boy of eleven to be still playing on a swing, but it was good somehow, just sitting there, swinging idly back and forward – a good time for thinking, and just being alive.

It was late in the afternoon – I'd done with my school work for the day, and I was filling in time before going to feed the chickens. I'd been swinging a bit more vigorously than usual, I guess – anyway, the rope one side broke, and tipped me onto the ground. Pain shot up my leg as I tumbled over, and I guess I must have yelled pretty loud. Next thing I knew, Mum was there, and so was Grim, the pommie hand who did most of the cooking for the men – I've mentioned him before, haven't I? They checked me over, and carried me back to the house. Grim drove into town for the nurse, and Mum radio'd the RFDS, 'cause they reckoned I'd have to go to hospital, and the nearest one is in Roma, too far to drive.

The nurse had just arrived and confirmed that I'd bust my ankle, when I heard the outside door open, and my Mum's voice in the kitchen:

'Oh, Cobbo, I'm glad to see you! Jack's had an accident.'

'What's happened? How is he?' There was a tone in his voice I didn't recognise then, but thinking about it later, it sounded almost like fear. She reassured him:

'It's not too bad, he's just broken his ankle. That damned old rope swing broke! The nurse is here, and the flying doctor're on their way, to fly him to Roma.'

'Oh, right!' There was no mistaking the relief in his voice, and despite the pain I felt a kind of boost because he sounded so concerned for me. Then he was there with me, kneeling beside my bed, reaching for my hand:

'Trying to fly again, boy? Serves yeh right!' But there was nothing but sympathy in his eyes.

They flew me to the hospital, where they fixed my ankle and plastered the lower part of my leg. I stayed in overnight, and then the local air service took me back to the town's airstrip, where Mum and Cobbo came to meet me. For a while I had to manage on my one good leg and a crutch, to the amusement of everyone. Most of the men treated me with a kind of humorous sympathy, but all I got from Cobbo was jibes about pirates – when he saw me, it'd be 'Ar, Jim lad!' or 'Pieces of eight!' in a kind of parrot voice. But it was his leg-pulling that did me most good, I think.

The man reached for the opened bottle on the cabinet by his side, the image in his mind of the tall skinny kid with his shock of ash-blond hair and laughing eyes, hobbling around with his plastered leg. It brought a smile to his face, but an ache to his heart...

It put paid to my driving practice and a few other things for a while, but at last they took the plaster off, and life went back to normal.

Winter came at last, too. A chill in the air in the mornings, bright clear skies all through the days and darker evenings. Life goes on pretty much the same as usual, whatever the time of year, and until that year I'd just accepted that without thought. I don't remember now just when it was that I woke up one night, as Cobbo shook my shoulder:

'Jack? Jacko-boy, you awake?' I rolled over, annoyed at the loss of a pleasant dream:

'Nnh?' It was not even light yet.

'Jacko – it's the most beautiful morning you ever saw! Get up and come with me, eh?'

'What?' He laughed quietly:

'Come on, get up!'

'All right – go 'way for a minute.'

I got out of bed and dressed quickly, wondering what on earth could be so important. In the kitchen, he just said:

'Get your boots on and come with me.' I did, and followed him over to the stables. There was a thin frost on the ground – people think of it as being hot out here in the bush, but the winter nights can get pretty cold, too.

'Out here where you live, winter's the most beautiful time of year, Jack. And first light is the most beautiful time of day, right? I love to get on a horse and just go out there and enjoy it, whenever I can.'

'I've seen it before, Cobbo! You didn't need to drag me out of bed...' I was still complaining. He gave me a serious look, and asked:

'Have you, Jacko? Have you _really_ seen it?' I nearly made a smart remark, but there was a kind of enthusiasm in his eyes which kept my fool mouth shut. I mentally shrugged my shoulders and followed him out of the door.

We saddled up quickly, and led the horses out into the daylight just as the sun was lurking below the edge of the horizon, its glow beginning to open the sky. I'm sure Brando was pleased to see me – he was the pony I always rode when I could, back then – and his eagerness cheered me up no end. I'll tell you more about Brando later. I followed suit as Cobbo mounted and led the way out of the yard into the open bush, towards the impending sunrise. We rode slowly, at a gentle walk, away from the house, in silence until he said softly:

'Look now, Jacko. Look around you. Breathe in the air, feel the chill of the night and the warmth of the sun as it strikes your skin. Have you seen this before?'

I looked around, felt the reality of the world around me, and shook my head:

'No, I guess not.' Sensing his feeling of wonder at the beauty of the nature that surrounded us, I began to see it myself. I'd never given it a moment's thought before – this was just the way things were, it was where we lived, how life was – but that day it was as if I'd never been there before, never watched the sun edge its way over the horizon, never seen its first rays lighting the tops of the gums and sliding slowly down them until the spinifex began to glow like Moses' burning bush in the Bible: 'It really is beautiful, isn't it?'

'This is Australia, Jacko. God's wonderful country.'

Sitting on my horse that morning, I began to see for the first time just how amazing, how incredible, our world really is. How much beauty there is around us, all the time, even if we don't take the time to see it. And I think I began to understand too just how wonderful life itself is and how lucky we are to be here, to be able to <u>see</u> the beauty all around us.

I guess that's something else that Cobbo gave me. He made me take the time to see the world as it really is, to appreciate the beauty and improbability of all that is around us, every minute of every day. The cold clear blue of a winter morning like that one, and so many others afterwards, when I would eagerly get up to ride with him in the dawn; or the blazing glory of an outback sunset; or the roiling of the clouds before the rains come and the burgeoning of green all around when they do. And so, so much more!

And at the same time, he gave me the wit to see how incredible life itself is, what an astonishingly wonderful thing my own body is, even. I hope that is something I'll never lose, however old I become, however long I live.

The old man laid the book on his knees, his eyes gazing sightlessly into the past as tears squeezed from them and ran unheeded down his weatherbeaten cheeks. The beer was all gone now, but he no longer cared – all that mattered was the battered old exercise book, and the words of the boy he'd known so many years before. He shook his head to clear his thoughts, and raised it to his eyes once more...

As winter shaded into spring, he'd get me from my bed maybe once or twice a week, to go and ride with him. Mum must have known, but we didn't talk about it – I guess I felt it was something private, my time alone with him, and with nature itself. Otherwise, life went on pretty much as normal.

I don't know how much more I want to write, how much more to tell – this is much harder than I thought it would be. The whole idea was to spill out the memories, to give them free rein in the hope they'd begin to leave me alone, but so far the opposite seems to be happening. But maybe it will work in the end, maybe once I'm finished it will ease my mind, and let me go on with the rest of my life. Even so, I'm not going to try and tell you every little thing that happened – it would take the rest of my life to do that, I think! And I don't think there's much point – there would be so much to tell, but all the little details would just get boring. Not that I expect anyone will ever read this. There are a few things I mustn't leave out, though.

Anyway, dear diary! Spring again – my birthday came around, and we had a bit of a party. The Millers came over on the Sunday, and my friend Mark from the town – his Dad owns the garage there. Mum laid on a barbeque, and we all had a pretty fine time. The four of us – me, Johnny, Mark and Cobbo – played cricket in the yard, against four of the other hands, and we beat them by about forty runs; and Cobbo supervised a shooting match between us three boys. I won that, and I don't think the others were letting me win, either, even if it was my birthday!

Cobbo had been with us a year then, all but. Soon it was a year for real – sometimes it seemed no time at all, and then other times it was as if he'd always been there. And I guess I just took it for granted that now he was there, he always would be; he seemed to be more than happy, settled in the work and pretty much part of our family.

Lambing was on us again, with all the commotion and stress, people up and about at all hours, the vet appearing on the doorstep at any time of the day or night. And then summer – the rains came early that year, so there was no repeat of the run-off pipe incident! But I guess I'd have known to take an umbrella along, anyway!

And two more months on, we were getting ready for shearing again. Mum let me go out with Cobbo and the men this time without so much as a word, and we'd soon got most of the mobs in and corralled in the sheds or the paddocks. The shearing gang arrived, and began to settle in – the evening before they were going to start, Cobbo decided to check out the old generator – it had been a bit reluctant to start once or twice before we went out mustering, and I don't think he trusted it. And of course it's absolutely vital at shearing – it's the only thing we've got to power all the equipment.

I tagged along with him, and Morgy, another of the men, came with us. They tried to get it going, but it wasn't having any of it. Over and over, they wound the starting handle, dropped the taps, and all it would do was cough despondently and stop again. Cobbo wasn't too pleased; and his mood hit rock-bottom when Morgy said that he'd had to give up on it a couple of days before:

'Why the bl...' I think he remembered then that I was there: 'Why the blazes didn't you tell me that before? Here we are, startin' shearing in the morning, and no flamin' genny!'

'Sorry, mate! It's been so damned busy 'round here...'

'Ah, what the heck! Go an' get me tool-roll, will yeh? And the big wrenches from the workshop.' Morgy sloped off, looking sheepish, and Cobbo turned to me as I asked him:

'Do you know what's wrong with it?'

'Yeah, I reckon so, Jacko. I've had a bit to do with these old Listers before. They're a darned good engine, pretty near bullet-proof, but they like to work hard, and this one spends a lot of its life just chargin' batteries and the like. We'll have the heads off, and take a look-see.'

Morgy came back with the tools, and Cobbo sent him to get his supper. I watched, fascinated, as he quickly began undoing nuts and bolts all over the old engine. In what seemed like a matter of minutes, he had all of the shrouding off and lying around him on the ground – it's an air-cooled engine, he explained to me as he worked, and you have to take the air ducting off first before you can get at anything much else.

Next he had the covers off the top, exposing all the valve gear, still telling me what he was doing, and what the various things that were coming into view actually did. Then he had a long bar in his hands, with a big socket on the end – a heave, and a loud crack, and he had a big nut turning on the cylinder head. He moved the socket on to the next – another heave, another crack, and that was turning too. Soon all the nuts on each of the three heads were loose, and he spun them off with his strong fingers, passing them to me as he did so along with the big washers that sat underneath each one:

'Keep 'em all somewhere safe, Jacko – we'll be up the creek without them!'

And then he was easing the first of the heads off, rocking it gently, sliding it up the long studs which had held the nuts and lifting it clear. He peered at it and grunted, and then held it out to me:

'Thought so, Jacko-boy. Coked up.' He shifted it in his hands so that I could look closely: 'See there? Where the valves sit in the head, you can see daylight around the edges. See?' I nodded. 'Diesel engines rely on compression for them to work, Jacko. As it comes 'round, the piston comes up and compresses the vapour, which makes it get hot. A mixture of air and diesel, right? Enough pressure, it gets hot enough, and bang! It explodes, sends the piston over the top and down again. But if there're leaks all 'round the valves, you haven't got enough pressure 'cause it's all leaking away, and no bang. Engine don't run.'

'What do we do to fix it?'

'We pop the valves out, clean up the heads so they fit tight again, put it all back together, and hey presto!' He gave me a big grin: 'At least, we hope so!' But he sounded pretty confident to me. He gave me one head to carry, and we took all three over to the workshop. There, he put one at a time into the big vice on the bench, used a lever to release the springs and took the valves out. Then, with an old chisel and some emery cloth, he carefully scraped all of the black, sooty stuff from the head and passed it to me to give it a final clean with more emery cloth. We were using a light oil to lubricate what we were doing, and the mixture of oil and carbon seemed to get everywhere! It was a warm night, and I took my shirt off because I was afraid of getting it dirty and incurring Mum's wrath.

As we worked, he told me again:

'These old engines, Jacko – they don't like runnin' light. This is what happens to 'em, see? They don't burn the fuel properly, and the unburnt stuff sticks to the metal inside the engine, and builds up until it stops it running at all.'

'Like happened here?'

'Yeah, that's right, boy.' He indicated the black gunge he was scraping off: 'That's almost pure carbon, Jack. What you need to do is to make sure that every now and then you put a real heavy load on the engine – switch on everything you've got around the place, to make the genny work as hard as you can. Then wind the governor up so the engine's goin' flat out – and watch the black smoke that comes out of it! Let that clear, and you know it's burnt off all the crap inside, right?'

We were in the middle of cleaning up the valves themselves – 'We'll just clean 'em up with emery, Jacko. They should be what they call reground into their seats, but we ain't got the time or the kit to do that' – when Mum came looking for me, wondering where I'd got to:

'Jack – there you are! It's late...' I turned to her, and saw her eyebrows shoot up: 'JACK! What do you think you're doing, young man?' I knew I was in trouble if she called me 'young man' – I looked down at myself, and realised that I looked a bit of a mess.

My arms were black halfway to the elbows, and the same black had somehow got smeared all over my chest, and, far worse, on the front of my jeans.

'Sorry, Mum...'

'Angie? He was just helpin' me' Cobbo stepped in to my defence, and she turned to him:

'Don't you make excuses for him! He should be in bed by now, and he knows it!' Cobbo held up his hands:

'This is important, Angie. If we don't get the genny fixed, we ain't shearing tomorrow. We're not far off now – let him stay and help? He's learnin' from this; he'll need to be able to do things like this for himself one day.'

'O-oh! – as long as he's making himself useful, and not just getting in a mess for the sake of it...'

'Thank you, Angie. He's being a real help, believe me.'

'Thanks, Mum!' She gave me a stern look:

'Don't you say a word, young man! And get yourself scrubbed clean before you get into bed, all right?' I just nodded, afraid to say anything else in case she changed her mind.

We quickly cleaned up all the valves, and then I watched Cobbo refit them into the heads. Then it was back out to the genny shed, with a couple of kerosene lamps, and we put the heads back in place. Cobbo tightened them down with the big wrench again – 'They oughta be tightened with a special bit o' kit that gives you the right tightness, called a torque wrench, but we ain't got one. I reckon this'll do...' – and then he put all the rest of the engine back together in what seemed like no time at all. He fitted the starting handle, and wound it over a few times, listening carefully:

'You hear that tick-tick, Jack? That's the injectors working – they squirt the diesel into the cylinders. Sounds like it's all working right – see those levers there?' He pointed to the compression tap on one of the cylinders, and I nodded: 'Right – when I say, you flip 'em over. Okay?' I nodded again, and he gave me a grin: 'Here goes, boy!'

He began to wind the handle over, faster and faster, over and over and over, until he had the engine spinning at quite a pace:

'Now, Jacko!' I flipped one lever over, and the engine gave a resounding bang – but it began to run on the one cylinder while he carried on swinging the handle:

'Next one!' I flicked the next lever over, and we had two cylinders going. He left off cranking it and flipped over the last compressor. We looked at each other, grinning from ear to ear, as the old engine settled down to run at a steady speed. It was blowing out a lot of thick smoke, but that soon began to clear and before long it was running as clean and smooth as I'd ever seen it.

'Good-oh, Jacko!'

'We did it, didn't we?'

'We certainly did, boy.' He put his arm around my shoulders, and I slipped mine around his waist – he gave me a squeeze, and then said:

'You'd better go 'n get cleaned up, Jack, before you get in any more trouble!' I headed for the house, leaving him to watch over the generator for a while, hearing him ease the throttle back as I walked away, tired but happy.

The man's eyes gazed into a distance only he could see as they lifted from the hand-written page. He was back in that warm summer night, watching proudly as the begrimed twelve-year-old staggered off across the yard, so tired he looked almost drunk: *Good times, Jacko-boy!* But the ache in his heart told him those good times were all done as he went back to his reading...

Then it was Christmas again – that year, I got a lot of new clothes. I'm a bit old for toys now, a bit more taken up with how I look, I guess, so I was really pleased – new jeans and shirts from Mum, and a pair of fine boots from Cobbo. They're really beautiful, soft leather, all tooled like real cowboy boots. A bit showy, maybe – but I loved them. Funny thing is, I'd had a similar idea for him – I'd got him a new belt. The old one he always wore was getting a bit tired, threatening to split in two around the holes, and Mum suggested he'd like a new one. She helped me pick it, one week at the store when I went into town with her.

He unwrapped it, and his eyes were shining as he looked at me – he's got these bright blue eyes, did I tell you? A bit like mine, I guess. Anyway, he gave me a big smile:

'Hey, that's a real beaut! Thank you, Jacko-boy!' I was standing there, already wearing my new boots; he put his hand out, and I took it – but then he pulled me into his arms and gave me a big hug. I don't know if I've ever been so happy...

Mum had done her usual thing with dinner. It was quite late when we sat down to eat, the evening getting cooler, the sun slipping below the horizon. I'd rather have a bit less, if I'm honest – a barbie would do me fine – but she likes to do the Christmas Dinner thing properly, as she sees it! I don't mind the turkey and the stuffing, the roast potatoes – but I hate brussels sprouts! They really do make me feel sick – but she still insists on putting a couple on my plate, and makes me eat them. But – Cobbo was sitting next to me at the table, and when she wasn't looking, he reached over and speared one of them, popped it in his mouth.

'You actually <u>like</u> those things?' I whispered to him. He grinned, and shook his head:

'No! I hate 'em too – but we're mates, right?'

'Thanks, Cobbo!' Mum turned back to the table then, so we kept quiet for a minute – then, when she turned her back again, he speared the other one. He grinned at me as he munched, and swallowed hard:

'You can do me a favour with the dessert, right?'

'Okay' I said, puzzled. We finished the main course, and I helped Mum to clear away the plates, and sat down again while she got the pudding out of the oven. But when she served it up, he made an excuse to get up from the table for a minute. I tucked in – I love the old traditional Christmas pud! Then he was back – and as Mum turned away again for something, he switched plates with me:

'I can't stand dried fruit, Jacko' he whispered. I grinned at him, and quickly wolfed down his pudding, too. We shared a conspiratorial grin as Mum sat down again, all unawares of the tricks we'd been pulling under her nose!

This year, there was just Mum and me, and Grim, and one of the other men. It wasn't the same at all – I know Mum misses Cobbo, almost as much as I do. It's not just all the things he did around the station, how much he helped her to run the place, either. He always insisted that he was just one of the hands, but he was so much more, really – her friend and mine, and more even than that, certainly to me anyway.

There were bad times too, of course – but not many. One of the men, a ringer I wasn't too keen on, crashed the station's ute, wrote it off, and himself too, nearly. He got flown off to hospital, and we never saw him again. Mum took Cobbo with her into Roma, and they came back with a new Chrysler Valiant to replace the wrecked truck.

And that summer, during the rains, a little girl from the town went missing. All our men went to join in the search for her, and I went too, although Mum didn't want me too. We searched for a couple of days, but then they found her – she'd gone in the creek and drowned, fetched up a good few miles away, poor little kid. The funeral was a real sad affair – all the town turned out, of course, and I guess I'll never forget the look on her father's face as they lowered her down into the ground.

And there was Brando. I haven't told you about Brando, have I? Yes, I think I mentioned him before, didn't I? He was my horse – well, not really, I guess, because they all belonged to the station, but everyone thought of him as mine. He'd been born there, and I'd helped Abraham raise him when his mother rejected him. I was about eight then, and I remember getting up specially early to go and bottle-feed him, day after day. We got to be pretty close, and as he grew up I was the one, with Abraham, who spent most time with him. We always had a kind of special relationship – he'd recognise me and whinny if I came into the stables, and I swear there'd be a sad look in his eye if I saddled another horse. I'd ride him if I could, but he was kind of lightly built, not really suited to some of the heavier ground around the station. But fast! How he could go – I'd take him out on the track sometimes, just for the sheer joy of riding as fast as we could. And I'm sure he loved it just as much as I did.

Cobbo would come along, sometimes. He usually rode Jess, a long rangy mare with white socks, and she could go if she wanted to, as well. One Sunday we went out for a ride – we were a couple of miles from the house, going hell for leather, when a dingo appeared out of nowhere right by the track. He spooked Brando who tried to stop, but he kind of skidded and went over. I went up into the air and landed in a heap, winded but not hurt, thank goodness! Cobbo was there in an instant, bending over me to see if I was okay – I got up, feeling pretty shaken but with nothing broken, and ran over to Brando. He was lying on the ground – he tried to get up, but then gave it up and just lay there, looking at me.

'Brando! Brando – what's wrong?' I felt desperate – I knew he was hurt from the look in his eyes. Cobbo quickly looked him over; then his hand was on my shoulder:

'His leg's broken, Jack. Pretty bad.' I turned to him:

'You can fix it, can't you?' He shook his head. 'The vet, then! Get the vet!' He shook his head again:

'I'm sorry, boy, so sorry.' I'd been around horses all my life, and I knew what that meant, but I didn't want to accept it. He eased me to my feet and led me to where Jess was standing patiently:

'Look after Jess, okay? Hold on to her for me.' I took her bridle in my hand, and kept my eyes closed so as not to see what he was doing. When the crack of the shot came, I buried my face in her shoulder and wept.

Cobbo left me to cry for him; he knew the story, knew how close we'd been. But at last he got me up onto Jess, behind him, and rode with me back to the house, where Mum took over.

I still go riding, of course. I have to, at times – shearing, when I help to muster the sheep, of course, and for all kind of odd things that are needed to be done around the place. I ride Elvis usually, now – he's a neat pony, black with a big quiff over his eyes, which is how he got his name. He's pretty good – but he isn't Brando. And of course, I don't go riding for the sheer fun of it so much now. Every once in a while, I'll wake up early on a winter morning and sneak out to the stables. The dawn is a beautiful as ever, my breath and Elvis's misting in the cold air, but it's so lonely too. Perhaps that's the time I miss Cobbo most of all – I don't know why I do it, if it hurts so much, but sometimes I just feel like I have to. Maybe I'm clinging on to the memory – maybe I ought to try harder to let go, but somehow I just can't.

Late that summer, when the wet was almost over and the creek was high, the two of us went fishing again. It was something we'd do every now and again, when we felt like a quiet afternoon away from the house. Usually on a Sunday, when everyone normally had a day off and Mum would cook a big dinner for the evening, we'd take our rods and walk off somewhere close. Or maybe he'd take the ute and we'd go a bit further along. I loved that, because he'd usually let me drive! That day, we'd driven around three miles off, to where there was a bend in the creek and the water flowed slowly, even at that time of year.

We didn't have much luck, though. Both Cobbo and I had tried different places along the bank; I still wasn't getting any bites, and went to move a bit further along. I stepped onto a big flat stone, but it shifted under my foot. Something stung my ankle, and I caught a flash of glistening brown as the snake vanished into the undergrowth. I yelled, as much in fear as in pain, and Cobbo dropped his rod and came running:

'What is it, Jacko?' I'd sat down, and was holding my ankle in my hand:

'Snake – bit me!'

'What snake?' I bit my lip:

'Brown.' He must have seen the terror in my eyes – we were miles from home, miles from any help, and we both knew that a bite from a brown didn't give you that long. Out in the bush, without the anti-venom, it was a death sentence. He held my eyes, and said quietly:

'This is going to hurt, Jack. Just hang on and grit your teeth, okay?' Then he was sitting beside me – he took my ankle in his lap and looked at the two pin-points of blood. His knife was in his hand - I can still remember the flash as the sun caught it before I closed my eyes.

New pain slashed across my leg, and then he had his mouth to the cut, sucking and spitting, sucking and spitting. It felt as if he'd sucked about a pint of blood out of me before he stopped and peered at the wound again. He tied his handkerchief around my leg, a bit above where the bite had been, and then picked me up in his arms and almost threw me into the ute.

He propped my leg up on the dash, and the next thing I knew we were hurtling along, bouncing and leaping across the rough ground, making a bee-line for the house.

He slammed on the brakes, and without bothering to turn off the engine he was out of the car, lifting me in his arms again and yelling for Mum:

'Angie! Get on the radio! We need anti-snakebite serum, for a brown, right now!' She didn't stop to ask what had happened – I guess that bit was pretty obvious, really – but ran off to the radio. He dropped me on my bed, and then I heard him in the other room, on the phone:

'Hello – anti-venom, for brown snake – you've got some? – I'll be there right away!'

Then he was gone again, and I heard the ute scream off down the track towards the town. Mum came in to me, and sat beside me:

'The flying doctor's coming, Jack, they'll be here as quickly as they can. Where's Cobbo?'

'He was on the phone, to the nurse in town, I think. He's gone to get some anti-venom.'

'Oh bless him!' She was nearly sobbing, and I wasn't feeling too happy myself. But I was still alive, and still conscious – and that long after a brown bite I shouldn't have been. She turned and looked at my leg, and I heard her give a relieved gasp:

'Oh Cobbo, you darling! He cut your leg, did he Jack?' I nodded:

'Yeah. He sucked out a lot of the poison, I guess.' Never-the-less, my leg felt as if it was on fire, and I was still pretty scared, not sure if what he'd done was enough to save me, or if he'd just delayed things. Mum sat and talked to me, making me stay awake, until the ute slammed to a halt outside again and the nurse ran in, quickly followed by Cobbo.

'How's he doing?' She asked as she got the syringe ready. Then more pain as I felt the serum going in – she gave me another injection, and I heard her saying;

'I've given him something to knock him out for...'

I didn't know anything much for a few days, I guess. And I was pretty crook for a while after that, while my body got rid of the last of the poison. The nurse came by regularly, and she told me what had happened – the RFDS came and gave me a good looking over, and said that I'd be as well at home as anywhere else, so there they left me. And she told me that the doctor had said that it was Cobbo's quick action in getting most of the venom out that had saved my life. She said it would take a time for me to get right over it:

'The anti-serum is almost as nasty as the poison itself, Jack, and you've got to get that out of your bloodstream as well.' And she was right!

I was stuck in bed for days. It was a while before I felt like I could get up, but even then Mum kept me there despite my complaints. Cobbo came by every day – he'd come in and sit beside me, and talk about how his day had been and what was happening around the station. As I got better, I found myself feeling embarrassed when he was there, knowing that I owed him my life. I wanted to thank him, but how do you say thank you for something like that? What words are there that don't sound stupid, and completely inadequate?

But he was the one who raised the subject, kind of obliquely, when I was back to something like my old self. He fixed me with one of his rare serious looks:

'Jacko-boy – I know how you're feeling.' He held up a hand as I went to say something: 'It's what mates do, lad. Nothing to make a fuss over. Just make something of your life, be a good man – and I know you'll do that – and there's no more to be said.'

'But Cobbo – you...' He held his hand up again:

'Listen, Jack – someone saved my life, once. I never had the chance to repay him, but now I feel like that debt is settled, right? You might need to do the same, for someone else, one day. Now, that's the end of it, okay?' I just put my hand out, and he took it in his, smiling at me over it – we shook, and then he told me that Mum had said I could get up the next day. I leant forward, delighted at that news, and he gave me a tight hug.

After that, it wasn't long before life got pretty much back to normal. I got back to my chores around the house and the yard, and going out with the men when my help was needed. And my school work, of course! Looking back, I guess it wasn't really as long as it seemed that I was laid up, but at the time it felt like forever!

Autumn ran on, and before long winter was lurking just below the horizon. That summer, Cobbo and I had left off our early morning rides because he had to be out before sunrise most days, to avoid working right through the heat of the day. And even into autumn, he didn't come knocking for me as often as he had the year before – just once in a while, he'd wake me and we'd go and saddle up, and walk our horses out into the dawn. I didn't know why, and I didn't like to ask – our friendship hadn't changed any, I was sure of that, so I just took it that he had his reasons, even if I missed the time with him. If anything, the bond between us was stronger than ever – I took unconsciously to referring to him as my mate, after his words to me, and once, meeting someone we didn't know in town, that was how he introduced me: "N this is my mate Jacko...' He was just a part of my world, a permanent fixture around the station and in my life, so when the bombshell came, it was so much harder...

A feeling of tightness gripped the old man's heart as he lowered the book again. The words of an old song ran in his mind: *Yes, I've had a few regrets, too. None more than that, Jacko-boy – if I hadn't left you...* But he knew that living on 'if only's' was a waste of time, that looking back served little purpose: *But what else have I got now?* He was nearing the end of the exercise book, and dreading what he would read, but he steeled himself and raised it to his eyes once more...

It was the beginning of June. A clear morning, with light just softening the sky when he shook me awake:

'Comin' ridin', Jacko?' I was up like a shot, dressed and out into the yard. We saddled up, me on Elvis and him on Jess, and headed out at a slow walk across the open bush, our faces towards the horizon where the sun was waiting for us before it deigned to rise. I don't remember either of us saying a word – we halted side by side and sat there for half an hour or more, watching the sunrise, mist trailing from the horses' nostrils. The world was as beautiful then as I've ever known it, and I felt as if I was a part of the bush, a part of this wonderful land – for that little while, my name was Australia.

And then, without a word, we turned our horses and rode back.

The rest of the day passed me by without making any impact – just another normal day. But then after dinner, he put his hand on my shoulder as he got up from our table:

'Come with me, Jacko, I need to talk to you.' I stood up, puzzled, and followed him out into the yard. He led me to the far fence, and we sat side by side, gazing now into the sunset. It was a glorious evening, the sun going down in a blaze of red and gold, and again we sat without speaking for a while. Then he put his hand on my shoulder again:

'Jacko-boy – life is all about change, you know that, don't you? Everything moves on, the seasons change, we get older. Look at you – you're not the funny little kid I met when I came here, not any more. You're growing up, and you're going to be a fine man, I can see that.' He paused, and I felt the first flush of doubt, unsure of where this was going. He went on: 'We all move on, all through life, right?' Now my doubt was becoming fear – I think I sensed already what he was saying, and it struck me like a blow in the face. But he was still talking: 'It's time for me to move on, Jacko. Time for a new horizon, new challenges, new places.'

'No... No, Cobbo...' I was shaking my head in denial.

'Yes, Jacko-boy. I've been here now much longer than I ever intended. Remember what I told you, about why they call me Cobbo? I never stay around anywhere for long, always on the move, right? Now it's long past time for me to go.'

'No! You can't, Cobbo! This is your home too, you <u>belong</u> here! We need you!'

'I can, boy. More important, I must. It's long past time, Jack, and I've got to move on.'

'No... No! You've got to stay, please? I... I <u>need</u> you...' An idea struck me: 'You could marry my Mum, and stay with us – she really likes you, I know she does, I'm sure she'd want to if you asked her! And... And you could be my Dad, for real...' I was crying unashamedly now, but he shook his head:

'It wouldn't work, Jacko. Oh, sure, I think a lot of your Mum, and I know she likes me, but that's not enough. You should only ever marry for love, Jack, remember that. You'll know when it happens to you – wait for the right girl to come along, don't jump the gun for the first pretty face that appeals to you. Me and your Mum? No Jack, we like and respect each other, but love? No boy, we don't love each other.'

I just sat there dumb, staring at him; I'd run out of words. He put his arm around my shoulders now and drew me close, and I cried into the shoulder of his worn old shirt. At last he eased me to my feet and led me inside.

I didn't sleep much that night. I lay there, my mind whirling and screaming, trying to think of a way to make him stay, any way I could persuade him not to go and leave me alone. Nothing sensible came to me – all I could think of was to try again, to talk to him in the morning and make him see how much we would miss him, how much we depended on him. At last I guess I must have slept.

When I woke up, for a moment I couldn't remember why I felt so desperate. Then it all came back to me and I leapt out of bed, hauling on my trousers, determined to go to him and change his mind. But I was too late. Sometime in the night, he'd thrown his swag into that beat-up old Holden and driven off into the darkness. I sat on the step, my world in ruins, a huge empty hole where my heart used to be. Mum found me there later, my face buried in my arms. She gave me a big hug and held me so tight, but the emptiness wouldn't go away. It still won't.

What now? It's been nearly a year since he left, and took half of my life with him. Mum's been great, she's tried her best to make things better for me, but I know she misses him too, his company of an evening, his cheerful conversation, the way they would pull each other's leg and laugh over silly things. And my friends – Johnny, and Mark, I think they know how I feel even if I can't talk to them about it. They've been pretty good too, trying to cheer me up and take my mind off of things.

But the emptiness is still there. Every minute, every day. Maybe I don't want to remember, but I can't help it – going fishing, cricket in the yard, helping in his jobs around the house or out on the station, just the knowing he was there even when he wasn't with me. Most of all, sitting on a horse at his side, watching the sun come up to bring colour to the land and softly wipe away the frost of a winter's night.

I still don't know, don't understand, why he left. Where did he have to go, what did he have to do, that was so important that he had to leave us to manage without him, to leave me alone? I'm not sure if I believe in God – but I do believe in <u>something</u>, some power out there, beyond what we can see and understand. The world around us is too incredible, too beautiful, to have been just an accident – and it was Cobbo who made me see that, see how wonderful life is. Maybe that's why he left – was he sent to me, to help me grow up, to help me begin to understand what the world is all about? And when he thought that job was done...

He gave me so much. My life, after the snake-bite. He was the one who changed me from that funny little kid into the person I am now – can I go on to be the man he talked about without his help? I don't know.

I guess a lot of this is my fault. Maybe I shouldn't have let myself come to be so close to him, or to depend on him so much. I let him be the father I wanted, a substitute for the father I lost – and now it's me that's hurting. I should have known better – but it's too late, now.

Love? Is that a word I can use? Is it okay for a thirteen-year-old boy to say he loves a man who isn't his Dad, or even an uncle? What the Hell! I love you, Cobbo. I wish now that I'd said that to you while you were still around to hear me say it. Perhaps in some strange way I can still say it to you, wherever you are, whatever you're doing – I did love you, and I still do – and I think, no, I _know_ that you loved me too, Cobbo. Do you, still? Do you miss me, do you think of me, sometimes?

I know that I'll never see you again, but I'll never forget you. You're a part of me now – neither time nor space can ever change that. And maybe I'm part of you, too. If you can hear me, there's only one thing I'd ask of you: Wherever you go, whatever you do, Cobbo, remember me.

Remember me.

The old man sat staring at those last words. He drew a deep breath, let it out slowly in a long, shuddering sigh; he closed the book and laid it aside, its story told at last. He sat, his head bowed, his eyes closed, his face buried in his hands, for what might have been minutes or hours; but at last he roused himself and glanced at the clock on the unit beside the bed. He smiled ruefully to himself, aware of the exhaustion aching throughout his body: *You'd better try and get some sleep, Cobbo!*

He stretched out on the bed without bothering to undress, and folded his hands behind his head – but sleep would not come to him. Thoughts and memories chased each other through his brain like a pack of station dogs playing in the yard, each yapping at the heels of the last – he tossed and turned, trying to calm his mind enough for fatigue to drag him into slumber, trying to get the rest he knew his tired body needed. After an hour or more, he gave up the unequal struggle, and allowed his mind to replay all of the events of the previous afternoon and evening:

He'd parked the Falcon outside the Kananga Inn, climbed out and crammed the Akubra on his head. He'd strode off to the bar, swinging the car door shut behind him without bothering to look back, reaching for the pub door. It opened as he approached, and a tanned, middle-aged man in a checked shirt and jeans stepped out into the sunshine:

'G'day – how're yeh goin'?' He held the door open for the old man.

'Good, mate. Yerself?'

'Ah, pretty fine I reckon.' They exchanged smiles; the old man went on inside and the younger fellow walked over to his Jeep Patriot and climbed in. The engine started, and it roared out into the road and headed out of town.

In the shade of the bar-room, the old man took off his hat again and looked around. In the mid-afternoon of a working day, it came as no surprise to him to find the place deserted except for the bored-looking bartender. The barman looked up from his newspaper:

'G'day – what can I get yeh?'

'VB, if yeh got it mate.'

'Comin' up.' He reached into a cabinet behind him without getting off of his stool, twisted off the cap and slid the bottle along the counter to the man, who caught it deftly:

'Cheers!'

'Havin' more than one? I'll keep a tab for yeh.'

'Yeah, please.' The old man looked around him: 'You still do rooms here?'

'Yeah, sure. You stayin' for a while?'

'Day or two, maybe.'

'Right-o, I'll get the missus, she does all that.' The barman got off the stool and called up the stairs behind the bar: 'Martha? Man down here wants a room!' He turned back to the old man: 'I'm Robbie Gilchrist – Martha 'n me, we own the place. She'll look after yeh.' The man put out his hand:

'Farley – people call me Cobbo.' They shook as the woman appeared and smiled at the newcomer:

'You want a room, Mister...?'

'Farley, Ma'am. Yes, please, for a night or two, at least.'

'Well, we've got plenty! I'll put you at the back where there's a good view over the bush, shall I?'

'That'll do fine, Ma'am.' She took a ledger from behind the bar and began to fill in a fresh line. The man spoke up again:

'Maybe you can help me – I'm looking for someone who used to live around here.'

'Sure, if we can' the barman told him: 'What's the name?'

'Westrom. They used to have the Kananga Station, just out of town.' Gilchrist shook his head:

'Nah. No-one of that name 'round here.' But his wife interjected:

'Wait a bit, Robbie – there was a Westrom, had that place. Long time ago, mind, before you came here. A woman on her own – Annie, was it?'

'Angie' the old man corrected her.

'Ah, right! And a boy – she had a son, right?'

'That's right. Jack, Jack Westrom. I used to work for them, like you say, a long time ago. He'll be a grown man now, young Jack, pushin' fifty I guess?

'Yeah, I remember now, Martha – you told me the story.' The barman was nodding. His wife gave him a thoughtful look as her mind probed the past, and then turned back to the old man and asked:

'You were pretty close to them?' She'd seen it in his eyes.

'Yeah, you might say that. The boy, especially – he was kind of a protégé of mine.'

The woman exchanged looks with her husband as the memories came back to her:

'You'd better sit down, Mr Farley.'

'Cobbo – everyone calls me Cobbo.'

'Take a seat, Cobbo.' The barman pulled another bottle from the cabinet, took the cap off: 'That one's on me, mate.'

Martha left the half-completed ledger on the bar and came to sit opposite the old man:

'You knew Mrs Westrom and the boy real well?'

'Sure – I worked there for more than a year and a half; they were real good folks.' She nodded, her brow furrowed:

'For sure – I remember you! Cobbo, of course! I was just a little kid then – my Ma ran this place, Dad owned the bakery up the street...' She sighed, and there was sadness in her eyes: 'Yes. Angie Westrom. She sold up – can't have been so long after you moved on. There was a bush fire, wiped out half of Worrongatta – that was the neighbouring property, you remember?'

'Yeah, sure – the Miller's place, right?'

'That's right. They've still got it, too. But back then, they were hurting, lost a lot of the stock as well as the vegetation. Fire left Kananga pretty much alone, but – Mrs Westrom'd had enough, and they bought her out. Bank saw it as a good deal, combining the two stations, so they put up the money.'

'You saw the fella who left, just as you came in?' her husband interjected.

'Yeah?'

'That was Johnny Miller. He runs the whole shebang, nowadays. His folks are still around, still live on Worrogatta, but they're pretty much retired, now.'

'Johnny Miller?' There was surprise in the man's voice, and Martha smiled:

'Yeah. Jack Westrom's best mate, when they were kids. You'd remember him?'

'Sure! I never recognised him, though.'

She paused as if unsure how to continue, and glanced at her husband:

'Robbie here didn't know the Westroms – he came along a while later, when my folks were running this place. Married me to get his hands on it.' Her husband laughed, and the old man gave them a grin. She went on: 'Where did you go when you left, Cobbo? What have you been doing all these years?'

'Oh, here and there. I spent a year working for a Pommie couple over on Marloo Creek Station, up north of Mitchell, and then kind of worked my way further northwards, swapped sheep for cattle up around Rockhampton way. I've been working up at Weipa the last five years or so, driving trucks around the Aluminium mines up there. But I decided I'm getting too old for that – I gave it away last month, and thought I'd come back down here, see how folks were doing.' She could see in his eyes that he knew their conversation was skating around something: 'So what happened to Angie Westrom, and the boy?' She drew a deep breath:

'She went to live with the Millers, on Worrongatta, stayed there a long time. Then she moved out to Redland Bay, near Brisbane, where her married sister lived. Never remarried, or anything – I guess she hadn't the heart for it. She died a few years back, Cobbo – lung cancer got her. But she's buried here, in the cemetery – that was her wish. Her husband's there, of course – but I expect you knew that?'

'Yeah, of course. She'd want to be with him, I guess.'

'Yeah – right.' Martha hesitated now, and he saw the pain in her eyes:

'What is it, Martha?' His voice was gentle but expectant, and she found it hard to speak. At last she drew breath again:

'Jack's there too, Cobbo. Beside them.' He stared at her, disbelief and shock written on his lined face:

'Jack? Jack's *dead?*' She nodded:

'I'm so sorry, Cobbo.' She reached out and put her hand over his where they lay clasped on the table; his gaze slipped from hers, and his head bowed. At last he looked up at her again:

'How, Martha? What happened?'

'One Sunday afternoon – he was out somewhere with Johnny, just the two of them, and they were fooling around like kids do. There was an accident, Cobbo. Jack never made it.'

'When? You said kids – how old was he?' She squeezed his hands:

'Thirteen, Cobbo. He was just thirteen when he died.' The grizzled grey head shook, and he stared sightlessly at the tabletop:

'No... No – oh, *Jacko*...' Tears were running down the weather-beaten cheeks now, falling onto the battered wooden surface of the table. A hand rested on his shoulder, and a glass appeared in front of him:

'Get that down yeh mate. I reckon yeh need it.'

The old man downed the whisky in one shot, hardly feeling its warmth in his throat. Behind him, he was vaguely aware of the barman dialling, and speaking in subdued tones on the telephone. Then that sympathetic hand was on his shoulder again:

'Cobbo? Johnny's on his way over. I reckoned yeh'd want to talk to him, right?' He looked up to see the hurt in the barman's eyes:

'Yeah – thanks, mate. He was – with Jack?' he asked the woman.

'That's right, Cobbo. He can tell you what happened – I don't remember very much, it was so long ago now.'

'Yes – thank you. It's...' She squeezed his hands again:

'It must be hard – all these years, to come back now and find this...' He just nodded again, and fresh tears fell on the table as he sank his face into his hands.

Silence reigned in the near-deserted bar. Martha rose quietly to finish filling in the ledger, leaving details about the old man's home address and so on until later, leaving him alone to grieve for his lost hopes, the stubbie of beer forgotten in his hands. Robbie sat on his stool behind the bar, his paper forgotten, his eyes on Cobbo, his thoughts reeling, trying not to imagine what the other man was going through.

The afternoon drew on; soon, the evening's regular clientele would begin to arrive, eager to dampen their parched throats, to yarn about the day's unimportant happenings. The old man felt a hand on his shoulder again, and looked up, his mind struggling to return to the present:

'Have you eaten today, Cobbo?' He shook his head. 'I thought not.' A plate landed on the table in front of him, a knife and fork with it: 'Steak, egg 'n chips. Get it down you, you need to eat!' Martha admonished him as he tried to protest his lack of appetite. He began to eat, half-heartedly, only to realise how hungry he was. He finished the big steak, cleared the plate, but never tasted a single mouthful of it.

A couple of men came in, to sit at the bar with their stubbies, talking quietly after their initial cheery greetings to Robbie. The door opened again, and the man he'd passed as he arrived came back in, looked quickly around, and walked over to take the seat opposite him at the table and hold out a hand:

'Cobbo? You won't remember me, I reckon – Johnny Miller.' The old man shook the proffered hand with a thin smile:

''Course I do, Johnny – even if you were just a kid when I knew you.'

'Can I get you a beer? Or something better?' The grey head shook:

'No, I'm fine, Johnny. For now, anyhow.'

The silence was awkward, difficult, as the two men studied each other. Miller found himself lost for words, not knowing how to approach the reason he was there, half-afraid even to disturb his own memories. The barman brought a glass of beer over, put it down at Miller's elbow. Eventually, he held out the old manila envelope he carried in his other hand:

'This... It's for you, I guess. It's something Jack wrote, after... After you left.' The old man took it, looked at its worn, tattered edges, turned it over in his hands:

'You know what it says, Johnny?'

'More or less. I did read it once, but that was a real long time back. Must've taken him a while, he just about filled one of his school exercise books. His mother kept it for years, but she let me see it. Her sister left it with me after she died.'

'What is it, Johnny?'

'It's... It's about you, mostly. About the time you had together, how... How he felt about you. I guess it's yours now – I reckon he would have wanted you to have it.'

'Yeah... Thank you, Johnny.'

The silence now was a little less painful, their shared sorrow at least acknowledged. Cobbo broke the silence:

'Jack...' Miller's eyes closed momentarily, and he sighed:

'Jack. He was my best friend, when we were kids. We'd get together when we could, ever since we were toddlers. Our folks got on real well, so I guess it was kind of inevitable that we would, too. My Dad did what he could to help Mrs Westrom, after her husband died – she was amazing, keeping that property going on her own! O'Riley, the manager, he was great, too – but then he seemed to think he could do as he liked, twist things around to his own advantage. She caught him in the end, fiddling the books, raking off extra for himself. Sent him packin'. Then you came along, Cobbo.' He paused, took a deep breath:

'You did so much for them. Kept the place going, made her life so much better, so much easier. And you meant so much to Jack – he'd go on forever about the things you did with him, whenever we saw each other. He was really cut up when you left, Cobbo. He never understood why...' Miller raised a hand as the old man went to speak: 'It doesn't matter now, it's all long over and done, Cobbo.' He paused, drew breath again:

'And then...' His head bowed as he hesitated, momentarily unable to go on.

'You were with him?' Cobbo prompted gently; Miller nodded without raising his head, spoke to the table:

'I haven't thought about that day for a very long time. I guess I've tried, all this time, to forget it, to wipe out what happened – but I couldn't. He was gone, and I had to live with that, come what may.' He looked up, but his eyes were far away as he collected his thoughts. He took a long pull at his beer, put the glass down softly again on the table:

'We were at Kananga, me and my parents, my little sister. A hot, dry Sunday afternoon, even though it was late autumn – Mrs Westrom was doing dinner for us all, she and my Dad had got the barbie going in the yard. Jack and I had wandered off – we'd been shooting, potting rats around that old dump behind the bunkhouse, you remember? We'd got a few, then we got bored, I guess, and headed out into the bush a way. We were a mile or two off, by the side of the creek – it was pretty hot, and we splashed each other with water to cool off, laughing and fooling, you know? We'd both got our shirts off, and I remember thinking how brown he was – you remember how his hair used to get bleached in the sun so it was nearly white, made his skin look so dark? How his freckles would come right out?

'We sat down on the grass there, just talking about nothing much, the way kids do, I guess. For some reason, we got to scuffling – not a fight, just playing, you understand? I can't even remember why, now – usually, it was one of us taking the piss out of the other for something stupid, and it'd end up in a play-fight, both of us laughing and hollering, you know? But this time, we'd got our guns with us. We'd put them down by our sides when we sat down – and somehow, his got caught up with us as we were wrestling...'

His voice trailed off, and the old man looked at him, his own pain temporarily overtaken by the sympathy he felt for his companion. Eventually, Miller spoke again:

'Jack yelled at me to pack it in, that his gun was right there – but then it went off. He... He got the bullet, in his chest...' He broke off again, but then forced himself to go on with a visible effort: 'I ran, all the way, back to the house. Couldn't speak, by the time I got there, but they understood something had happened. I went with Grim, the Pommie hand who worked for them then, in the ute, to show him where... We brought him back – the nurse came out from town here, and the Flying Doctor, but it was way too late by then...' He stopped speaking, overcome by his memories, and covered his mouth with his hand, shook his head.

After a minute or so, he spoke again, his voice so soft now that Cobbo was straining to hear:

'They said later at the inquest that he'd died on the spot, that it'd killed him instantly. I've tried over all this time to convince myself that at least he didn't suffer, that he didn't have the time to feel anything – but it doesn't help, Cobbo. It doesn't help at all.'

Silence fell again between them. The murmur of voices behind them, the clink of glass, the hiss of the beer pumps, failed to penetrate their shared sorrow. Their hands met on the table, clasped, held.

At last the old man asked one more question:

'His gun, Johnny?' Miller looked up into the pain-filled blue eyes:

'Yeah. He was so proud of that gun. It was an air-rifle, a real beaut. He'd had it as a Christmas present, I think? A year or so earlier...' Sudden realisation dawned in his eyes: 'Ah, *Christ!* You...?'

The tears were running unheeded down the old man's face now:

'That's right, Johnny.' Anguish shone in the bright eyes that held Miller's horrified gaze:

'That's right. That boy was the closest thing to a son I ever had – and I gave him the gun that killed him.'

***

The old man rose early the next morning. He'd given up any attempt at sleep, trying merely to let his body rest while his mind churned on and on, trying to come to terms with all that fate had thrown at him through the previous day. At last he gave even that up just as the dawn was trying to loosen the grip of night upon the vastness of the outback. He pulled on his boots, threw on his jacket and stole quietly out of the pub's front door, cramming the old Akubra on his head. The night's shower of rain had long passed – the sky now was a clear, deep blue, shading to soft pink where the sun hid its face just below the distant horizon.

He had arrived with a quest, but now he felt lost and directionless, like a ship without a rudder. He gazed into the widening sky, feeling in his soul the rotation of the Earth, remembering mornings long ago, astride a horse in the dawnlight, a boy at his side; and Jack's words came back to him: *For that little while, my name was Australia...*

The keys were in his pocket, but he scorned the shiny new truck and set off afoot along the half-mile of the main street, turned into Charles Street at the end, and so to the gates of the cemetery. He paused on the threshold:

We came here once together, Jacko-boy, do you remember? You, me and your Mum. She usually came alone, but that one time... You two stood there, after she'd tidied his grave and laid her flowers, hand in hand – and then you turned to me, held out your other hand with that look in your eye – and I took it and stepped up to be beside you, although it wasn't my place to be...

The old man walked slowly along the dry, dusty path, around to the far corner, where three stones stood side by side, and halted, gazing at them. The first, clean, bright and new, next to the boundary fence:

> ANGELA JANE WESTROM
> BELOVED WIFE OF ARTHUR...

Beside it, bearing the tarnish of time:

> ARTHUR WESTROM
> THE LORD HATH GIVEN, AND THE LORD HATH TAKEN...

And the last. He could barely see the words for the burning behind his eyes:

> JACK WESTROM
> AGE 13
> YOU SHALL NOT GROW OLD...

He sank to his knees, bowed his head for a moment and then looked up again:

'Hello Jack.' He spoke softly, gently, and paused to bring his thoughts into some kind of order: 'You have no idea how often I've dreamed of saying those words, Jacko-boy. How often I've come so close to just giving it all away and getting in the car, coming back here to find you. I've wondered what you'd say, what you'd do – would you shake my hand, give me a hug? Or would you still be angry, would you have a go at me for going off and leaving you like that? Even your anger would be so much better than this...' He bowed his head again, tears squeezing from between closed eyelids to dampen the red earth, emptiness gripping his heart.

'I should have got some flowers, I suppose. That's what you do, isn't it?' He gave a snort of ironic laughter: 'What would you have thought of that, eh Jack? Flowers, for a teenage boy! Hardly the thing to do, is it?' He paused again, the hollow feeling in his chest getting stronger: 'This was the one thing I never imagined, Jack – that I'd come back to find you gone. Moved on, maybe – that's what I've spent my own life doing, Heaven knows! But dead? Never, Jack, never.' He drew a shaky breath:

'What now, Jacko? I've got no more dreams now, boy. You were the last of them. I've read your story, too. You were right, all along – I did love you. And like you I never lost that love – through all the years you were there in my heart, I never forgot you. How could I? And I never will, Jack. I've abused this old body a lot, over a long time, and I don't know how much longer it'll put up with me, but however long I remain on this earth, I can truly promise to do what you ask, Jacko. I will always remember you.'

The tide of grief and loneliness that had been lapping at his heart rose up to engulf him as he reached out to touch the boy's headstone...

***

It was Johnny Miller, come to tend the Westrom plots along with his own family's later that morning, who found the old man, lying as if sleeping beside Jack Westrom's grave, his arm outstretched across the earth as if to embrace the long-dead boy.

And it was there at his side, a week later, that they laid him to rest.

The bar of the Kananga Inn had never been so quiet, at least not during opening hours. And it was far from empty; much of the town was there, all in their Sunday best rig, and the beer was flowing, if not profusely, then in a steady fashion. No-one had anything to say, until a hushed question rose from an anonymous throat:

'There gonna be a stone fer 'im?'

'Yeah. His cousin's payin' for it.'

'Didn't know 'e'd got a cousin?'

'Too right! Back in the UK. Turns out he's a lord, or an earl, or somethin'.'

'What – Cobbo?'

'No, you mongrel! The cousin.'

'Strewth!'

'What're they puttin' on it? The stone, I mean?'

''Is name, I reckon.' The words were heavy with irony.

'Ah. Anyone know what it was?'

'Yeah. On an old passport, in 'is swag. Lennox Farley.'

'Lennox? What kinda poncy name is that?'

'English I s'pose. If your cousin was an earl, you might be called Lennox!'

'Yeah. Scary, ain't it?'

'Cobbo. Everyone knew 'im as that, didn't they? Put that on 'is stone.'

'Yeah, too right.'

A thoughtful pause.

'More beer, anyone?'

'Good on yeh, Robbie!'

A shuffling of feet and glasses as the drinks were replenished; then another voice:

'Heart attack, did they say?'

'Yeah, s'right mate.'

'Yeah... 'Ow old was 'e, anyone know?'

Martha looked up from the dark-n-stormy cradled in her hands:

'I reckon 'e must'a been 'round forty when I was a kid, when 'e was here before. What do yeh think, Mark?' The garage owner grimaced;

'That'd be 'bout right, I guess.'

'Makes 'im knockin' on eighty, then.'

'Seventy-five, any'ow.'

'Yeah... No big surprise, then. I mean, drivin' all the ruddy way down from Weipa, 'n then the disappointment when 'e got 'ere...'

'Yeah – too much fer a dodgy 'eart, eh?'

'Broken heart, more like' Martha suggested.

'Crikey, yeah! Can you imagine, all that time, to dream about comin' back 'n lookin' for the kid, only to get here and find out he'd been dead all along?'

'Yeah...'

'Wonder why he upped 'n left like that?'

'Gawd knows. I could never make that out – he thought the world o' Jack when we were kids, I remember' Krascjyk shook his head in puzzlement: ''N Jack worshipped 'im. 'E was so cut up when 'e went...'

'Guess we'll never know. Mebbe thought he was gettin' in too deep – some fellas just can't handle havin' roots, know what I mean?'

'Came back in the end though, didn't 'e?'

Sadness echoed in the silence. Then another voice from the crowd:

'Still, 'e foun' what 'e was lookin' for, didn'e?'

'What do yeh mean, mate?' The response was slightly scandalised.

'Well – if what they tell us is right, he's with 'em again now, ain't he? Him, 'n Angie, 'n young Jack. They'll be together again, right?' A rather stunned silence:

'Yeah. S'true, ain't it?'

'Christ, I hope so!'

'I'll drink to that...'

In The Snow

Winter came early this year. It's still a few days before Christmas, and I'm standing by the lake, the snow up over my shoes, watching the ducks and geese skating and sliding on the frozen water, a bitter breeze blowing around my ears. There is humour in the antics of the birds as I scatter breadcrumbs for them, but as always in weather like this, my mood is sombre.

Here in the snow, I cannot but think of you. It is so long ago, but I still recall winter days in the Taunus mountains, running and laughing, throwing snowballs at each other, you a lovely young girl wrapped up in your thick coat and bright scarf, me, what, five or six years old? Father was alive then; he would take us out into the forests on a Sunday afternoon to play in the snow – such fun we had! And again, in Prague, after we went to live with Tante Brigitte, away from the fear of the Nazis; the three winters we had there will live in my memory as long as I do, in her enormous garden, building snowmen, laughing and playing with our friends. Father never did come to join us.

You were as much mother to me as elder sister. Maybe you were only four years older than me, but you always seemed so grown up. You took care of me, saw that I wanted for nothing that was within our reach; you were really the one who made me the person I am. Father was always working, and his housekeeper kept so much to herself; and our maiden aunt, though a loving old lady, had little idea how to deal with a growing boy.

Being Jewish had no meaning for me as a child. Father was far from devout, and I hardly knew what it meant; we just got on with our lives, the same as everyone else. Even when he sent us to Tante Brigitte I don't think I really understood why, just that he was, for some reason, worried about our safety. After all, I was barely eight years old, and politics meant nothing to me. It was only later that I began to realise that something was wrong, when the people of Prague turned against us after Hitler annexed the Sudetenland.

It is not just the cold and the snow, the winter here in England. I have been there; I have seen the place where you died. It was winter then, too – a strange time to be playing the tourist, perhaps, but somehow appropriate. Tourist? Can a place of such unspeakable horror be called a tourist attraction? I wonder about the motives of some of those who might wish to go there – but I am glad that it has been saved, if only to remind us all, and the generations to come, just how unutterably cruel man can be to his fellowman. And, I hope, to ensure that it can never happen again.

I thought of you then, of course. Standing in the snow, seeing around me the last scenes you ever saw, the huddled shapes of the buildings softened by winter's blanket, the wrought-iron gates with their awful motto: *Arbeit Macht Frei.* How many were ever made free from that place? Pitifully few – only those who saw the Russian army break down those gates. The others from my coach wandered around, staring, pointing, their voices mercifully hushed, and I wondered if any of them had any connection with the place, any deeper reason than curiosity for being there. But it wasn't a thing to talk about – I felt no urge to tell them about you, and if they had lost loved ones there, they too chose to keep it to themselves.

And those old cine films. We've all seen them, on the television – the trains of cattle-trucks grinding in through those gates, the pinched, scared faces of the people herded out of them. And I suppose we've all felt the same horror at those scenes, known the heart-rending feeling that comes with the knowledge that few if any of those we see had more than hours to live. So many! The faces of the children are etched on my mind – that little boy, he could have been me... That girl, pretty despite her fear, so much like you...

How long were you there, my darling sister? I've never known for sure what happened to you, only the rumour that you were taken there, three years after you sent me away to England. Did you live in those terrible barracks, go to work in one of the Nazis' factories? Or were you one of those who went straight to the gas-chambers? Sometimes I pray that that was what happened to you, that you didn't know too much of the horror – you were a very attractive girl, a teenager, and I shudder at the thought of the things that could have happened to you. I remember you as I last saw you at the station in the summer of 1939, standing there in that pretty blue dress as you waved me goodbye, the steam from the train curling around your shoulders. But in my mind's eye I can see you there, too, standing in the snow with those awful buildings behind you, the smoke from the furnaces drifting off on the bitter wind, shivering in that same lovely dress, your sorrow and fear dulling your blue eyes.

But enough! Time to go home, back to the warmth of my little house, to think about what I am going to cook for my supper. I am an old man now, eighty-two years old – but maybe life has been good to me. I have my health, apart from the occasional twinge from my back and the odd bout of indigestion; I still get out quite a lot, even in the cold weather, and I enjoy my walking. I am alone, and perhaps that is a sadness – I did marry my sweet Barbara, only to lose her to cancer so soon after. We had no children, and I have no other family; but I am content, for the most part.

My surrogate parents, the English couple who took me in and brought me up when I arrived here, were childless themselves – I think that was why they were so eager to take on three little orphan boys from Czechoslovakia! So I have no foster-family either; and the other two boys and I lost touch later in life. We grew up and went our separate ways – not related, we had no deep reason to keep in touch, I suppose, although we did exchange letters for a while. They are both gone now, anyway – and I suppose it will not be so very long now before I follow them. After the war, I changed my name – Berndt Grunwald sounded, I thought, rather too German for a young man in post-war England, so I became Bernard Greenwood.

So I turn my footsteps homewards, away from the lake, up the slope to the road, cross over and into the backstreets of the estate where I live. There are few people about; I pass a near neighbour and we exchange comments about the weather. A car passes me – not many are out driving in this, either – and turns at the end of the road. I walk on, and then the car is back, going slowly; a smart black Mercedes Benz saloon with a new registration number. It pulls up alongside me and the window purrs down; I stop politely, expecting to be asked for directions:

'G'day – can yeh help me? We're lookin' for Ashburn Grove.' The accent is distinctly antipodean.

'Yes, of course! That's where I live – just go to the end here, turn right, and then second right, and you're there.'

'Yeh live there yourself?' The man is looking at me with a strange, doubtful expression; I guess him to be around fifty. He goes to speak, thinks better of it, but then tries again:

'Pardon me – but yeh wouldn't be mister Greenwood? Bernard Greenwood?' It is my turn to be puzzled now – why would they be looking for me? But:

'Yes, I am.' I see his eyes widen, and then a look of amazed surprise fills them as he turns to the lady at his side:

'Hey Debbie, we've found 'im! It's 'im!' The next moment he is out of the car, gazing at me as if I am something wonderful, standing in its open door, and I'm looking back at him, not sure what to make of his dramatic announcement. The lady has got out too, and she is looking at me over the car's roof with an amused smile on her face – she is, I suspect, quite a few years younger than him:

'Yeh've just made his day, Bernard!' Her tone is dryly cheerful.

'What – who are you? Do I know you?' I'm looking at the man more closely now, and there is something about him, something familiar. The excitement is clear in his eyes:

'Yeh had a sister, when yeh were a kid, right? Helga, Helga Grunwald?'

'I... I did – but how do you know that?' He laughs:

'I should know – I'm her son!'

'But... That's not possible! She's dead, she died in Auschwitz!' He's shaking his head now:

'No, she never went there. They kept her hidden in Prague, and after the war she got out of the country, made her way to Aus. Australia. She thought you were dead! They were told that your train had been stopped and all the kids taken by the Nazis.'

'She's alive?' Although I cannot believe anything of what he is telling me, the hope is there in my heart. But he shakes his head again:

'No, sorry – she died a few years back. But she always told us about you, about her little brother, how much she loved you and missed you after that English guy got you and all the other kids out of Czecho.'

'How did you find me?' I am still utterly bewildered at this turn of events, not sure I can believe my ears.

'Never mind, that's not important right now, we'll tell yeh later...' In the grip of a dream, I interrupt him:

'You're her *son?*' He just nods, and suddenly there are tears in his eyes:

'Yeah – I'm yer nephew. Me name's Frank, Frank Costan. She married an Aussie, yeh see.' And his arms are around me, threatening to crush me in a bear-hug. My nephew! My arms are around him too, still disbelieving but so full of joy.

After a moment he releases me, looking a bit shamefaced at his emotional demonstration, and waves at the lady who is watching us with that amused look in her eyes still:

'This is my wife, Debbie:' She waves across at me now, grinning: 'And the kids – hey, Luke, Kalina, get out here an'' meet yer uncle!' One back door of the car opens, and a young boy gets out looking slightly weary:

'Kal's asleep – again!'

'Never mind, we'll get her up in a minute. They're both whacked after the flight' he explains to me: 'Luke, this is yer Grandma's brother, that we've been lookin' for!' The boy looks up at me, and my heart leaps – if I needed proof, here it is: Big blue eyes, freckles, and heavy, glossy dark hair. He stares curiously at me:

'Uncle Bernard?' I can't speak, so I just nod. He holds a hand out, and I take it: 'It's good to meet yeh, Uncle.'

'You too, Luke – you have your Grandmother's eyes...'

'Yeah, so Dad keeps tellin' me!' He sounds world-weary - I reach out and take his other hand:

'How old are you, Luke?'

'I'm eleven – Kalina's eight, yeh'll see her if she ever wakes up! Yeh're really our uncle?'

'Yes, I am.' That truth suddenly hits me, and I cannot help myself – I pull the boy into my arms and hug him; he stiffens for a moment, but then I feel him relax, and his arms creep around my waist:

'Uncle Bernard...' The pretence is over. After seventy years, I have found myself again as well as the family I didn't know I had:

'Berndt. My name is Berndt...'

He leans back in my embrace and raises those bright eyes to mine, his smile lighting them:

'Uncle Berndt...'

Graduation Day

'Mark, you take Steph for a drink in the bar. I'm going up to the room to shower and get changed. I won't be long, and then when Danny gets here we can all go in for dinner together.' I leant forward to kiss my wife on the cheek; she turned with a grin at our companion and headed for the lifts across the hotel foyer. We were in the Randolph Hotel, in Oxford, celebrating Daniel's graduation from Keble College.

'Come on Steph. What'll you have?' I led the way around into the plush ground-floor bar and escorted the girl to a vacant table.

'Can I have a pint of Theakston's, or do you think we'll get thrown out?' I chuckled at the laughter in her eyes:

'You have whatever you want, girl! If they don't like it, that's their problem.' I walked up to the bar and caught the barmaid's eye: 'Two pints of Theakston's, please. Can you put them on a tab for me? My wife and son will be joining us soon.'

'Of course, sir. Where are you sitting?' I indicated our table: 'I'll bring your drinks right over for you, sir.'

'Thank you.' I went back to join Daniel's girlfriend.

'Thanks. No trouble from the natives, then?' I shook my head, laughing:

'No trouble, Steph! I expect they're used to the odd ways of students around here.' She grinned at me:

'Yes, I'm sure they must be. Especially every year when the graduation ceremonies take place! I expect a lot of bars around the town are battening down the hatches as we speak. Mr Andrews?'

"Mr Andrews!" - Stephanie was a rather old-fashioned girl in a lot of ways, and had always insisted on that rather formal way of addressing me. Perhaps that was one reason why Janey and I thought so much of her, were so pleased to welcome her as our boy's girl. But now there was an almost nervous tone in her voice:

'What is it, Steph?'

'Did you know... Dan's asked me if I'll marry him. Not yet, perhaps next year when I've graduated too.' I sat back in my chair:

'Oh my goodness, that's awful!' She stared at me, wide-eyed, and I burst out laughing: 'Sorry, Steph! But you ought to see the look on your face – it's priceless!' Her smile slowly returned as I went on: 'He hasn't told us, but it's no surprise. I think his mother's been expecting it for a while now.'

'You – you don't mind?'

'Mind? We're delighted! At least, I am, and I know Janey will be when we tell her. Steph, you've just put the crowning touch on what has to be the proudest day of my life.' She was beaming now:

'Thank you, Mr Andrews!'

'And if you're going to be my daughter-in-law, you'd better start getting used to calling me Dad. Or Mark?'

'Oh, yes, all right – Dad! And you're really okay about it?'

'Okay? Dan's mother and I think the world of you, Steph, and if you two want to spend the rest of your lives together then that suits us just fine. We're so proud of Dan, and we'd love to see you by his side.' There was a delightful shyness in her smile as she bowed her head slightly in acknowledgement of my reassurances. She looked up again:

'Mr Andrews – Dad – you know, Dan is so proud of you, too? I know you've had your differences, when he was a teenager, but he rates you somewhere between God and Superman!' I must have looked startled at this because she laughed suddenly: 'It's true! He's so pleased that you and he get on so well now...' She gave me a frank look: 'I had my rows with my parents too, when I was in the sixth form – I think it's something all teenagers do, isn't it? But we get on fine now as well – I think it has to do with leaving home, not being all crammed into the same space all the time, don't you?' She was probably right, I reflected; certainly, my relationship with my stepson had improved out of all recognition after he'd left for Oxford. She was still talking:

'He really admires you – and he never gets tired of telling people how you saved his life when he was a kid. I've lost count of the times he's told *me* about it!'

Our beers arrived, and if the barmaid disapproved of beautiful young girls drinking pints of ale, she kept her expression diplomatically neutral. In the few moments as she placed our glasses on the table, my mind had slipped reluctantly back in time...

I had been pleased, and I suppose quite proud too, that the little boy had survived his terrifying ordeal, even if the memories it evoked in me were so deeply painful. And that encounter had led me to where I am today, to meet his relieved but anxious mother when she asked the policewoman to bring me around to their house a couple of days later.

I had never married, never wanted children, the memory of my little brother still burning in my mind; but somehow

Janey and I had just fitted together from that first meeting. A crusty old batchelor – not so old, perhaps, I was only forty-four then – and a struggling single mother, trying to cope with bringing up a youngster on her own after his father had died of a sudden stroke at just thirty years old. And as our friendship had grown, to blossom into something so much stronger, so much better, the boy himself had crept inevitably into my affections until he had truly become the son I had never had. At first, I had thought his attention to me was just the result of his gratitude, of respect for what I had been able to do, but I soon realised that he actually enjoyed my company and wanted me with him, whether it was helping with his homework or kicking a football around in the garden or down the park, or just sitting beside him to watch television. And he'd seemed delighted to take my name when I adopted him officially, soon after his mother and I had married.

It was pure happenstance that I was there that day. I'd decided upon a prolonged lunch break from the shop, for no particular reason other than that trade had been slow and I was feeling rather down. I took my sandwiches and flask in the car and drove to the seafront; I parked looking out to sea and sat there munching quietly, watching the light clouds drifting across the autumn sky, enjoying what was a fine day for October, not cold, with just a light breeze blowing. It was half-term week and I'd seen the group of kids playing on the sand without taking any notice of them – normally, I avoided such things, the sight and sound of children stirring feelings I would have preferred to forget, but there they were, and I didn't feel like moving on elsewhere.

I ate my sandwiches, washed down with coffee from the flask, and then just sat there enjoying the tranquility of the scene. Until a sudden hullabaloo roused me from my contemplations – a little girl was hammering on the door of my car, tears streaming down her face:

'Help! Please, mister, help – it's Danny, he's hurt himself!' I wound down the window and she reached in to grab my arm: 'Help us, please mister, help us!'

'What is it, what's happened?' The panic was clear in her eyes:

'It's Danny, my friend – he's hurt bad, real bad! Please help?' I opened the door and got out of the car; she grabbed my hand and dragged me, running down onto the edge of the beach where they had been playing among the grass-topped dunes above the high-water line. Three other children were standing around there, looks of horror on their faces, obviously scared and panicky; one of the boys looked up as we approached:

'It's his leg, he's cut it real badly!'

The little girl hauled me along at the run until I could see for myself – a little boy lying on the sand, holding the top of his left leg in both hands, blood pouring from between his fingers. He raised terrified eyes to me as I asked:

'What happened?'

'I – I fell over. This piece of glass, it went right into my leg. I pulled it out, and it started bleeding...' He sounded breathless, gasping, and my memory reeled back thirty-two years. But this was not the time for dwelling on the past, however painful – I forced my mind back to the present. I looked around the other children:

'Who lives nearest?'

'I do.' It was the boy who'd spoken before.

'You have a telephone at home?' He nodded. 'Run home and telephone for an ambulance. Quickly now!' He nodded again and ran off, and I turned back to the lad on the ground:

'Help will soon be here' I reassured him, but the look in his eyes was as scared as ever. I looked up at the others again:

'Does anyone know where he lives?'

'I do.' The little girl spoke up.

'Then run there and get his mummy or daddy, bring them here.' She scurried away. A moan from the boy on the ground forced me to look down again – his short trousers were soaked in blood now, and more was running from where his hands were clasped to his leg, and my memory was screaming at me that he was going to die, just like Sammy, if I didn't do something...

I felt that same old panic rising in my chest again, just as it had then – but this time I was an adult, there had to be something I could, should, do for this kid. I dredged my mind for anything that might help – I'd never had any formal first-aid training, but something about bleeding and pressure points stirred in my brain. I knelt at his side and forced myself to take a closer look at his injury, gently lifting his hands away – the vicious shard of glass had clearly struck deeply into the inside of his thigh about a third of the way down. It had to have cut the artery there, from the amount of blood escaping in sharp spurts, and somehow I had to stop that bleeding, or at least slow it enough for the ambulance to get there. How long did I have? Minutes, at the best...

I took a deep breath and put my hands on his leg, suddenly aware that touching a little boy just there under any other circumstances would be likely to get me locked up. I moved my hands around, pressing hard against his flesh through the thin fabric of his shorts, feeling for the artery but not finding it. The blood was still pouring out of him, and the fear of watching him die was making me panicky all over again – but then, as I pressed hard in one spot, the flow of blood slowed noticeably. I gave a sigh of relief, eased my hand and then pressed harder, and it slowed even more, to the slightest trickle.

Keeping up that pressure, I carefully shifted myself into a more comfortable position, forcing myself to take a series of deep breaths to calm myself. The boy was gazing up at me, his eyes still wide and scared, and his other friends were standing a little back, watching us. Ignoring them, I gave the boy what I hoped was a confident smile:

'You're Danny, is that right?' He nodded. 'My name's Andrews, Mark Andrews. I'm pleased to meet you, Danny.' He was still staring at me, but I caught the faintest hint of a smile on his face only to see it vanish again under his fear:

'Thank you, for helping me...'

'You're welcome, Danny. How old are you?' I tried to keep his mind from his pain with conversation.

'I'm nine. I'll be ten in November.' My heart gave a jolt - Sammy had been eight when he died.

'Am I... going to be all right?' My attempt at distraction had failed.

'Yes, of course you are.' He didn't reply straight away, and the terror was back in his eyes:

'You're sure? I – I'm scared, I don't want to die...'

Those words! Suddenly I was twelve years old again, holding my little brother in my arms. We'd been playing down by the railway yards, on the derelict ground there, and, just like little Danny he'd taken a tumble. In Sammy's case, a piece of discarded metal had gone into his neck, and just like Danny it had severed the artery. Our older sister had set off to run home for help, leaving me to look after him – but I had no idea what to do to try and stop the bleeding. All I could do was to hold him and try to comfort him:

'I'm here Sammy, it's going to be all right...'

He had lain there in my arms, blood soaking his shirt, that same terror in his eyes, dark grey just like Danny's. He'd said that too:

'I'm scared, Mark – I don't want to die...' You're not going to, I told him, I won't let you – but in the end, I couldn't stop him. He'd reached up to me, stroked my face with his fingertips:

'I'm cold, Mark, so cold...' I hugged him tighter to keep him warm; and then his hand fell away as I watched the light fade from his eyes.

My father had arrived moments later, to find me clutching my brother's body to my chest, rocking back and forth on my heels, sobbing uncontrollably.

And now history was repeating itself. I suddenly realised that tears were streaming down my face again now – but this time I wasn't going to let this kid die in my arms! I'd all but stopped the bleeding, and he was going to make it. He had to make it!

'You're going to be just fine, Danny, nothing's going to happen to you, not while I'm here.' And the look of trust in his eyes wrung my heart. Sammy had trusted me, and I had let him down – but not this time! This kid was going to live, come what may...

And then the ambulance was there, and I could stand back, leave it to the professionals. They'd rushed him onto a stretcher and whisked him away; his mother had arrived just in time to go with him, and in the bustle I had got away with simply leaving my name and address with the policewoman who'd turned up with the ambulance. Two days later she'd knocked on my door and asked if I would go with her to meet the boy's mother – and eighteen months later Janey and I had married.

A hand on my arm brought me back to the present:

'Are you all right, Mr... Dad?' I looked up with a smile:

'Fine, Steph! Sorry – I was miles away for a moment.' She didn't look convinced, a concerned expression in her eyes. I took a deep breath:

'Has Dan ever told you about my brother? He had an accident, so much like Daniel's, when he was eight years old. He died in my arms – I was twelve, and I couldn't save him...' I averted my eyes, aware of the tears burning behind them, and she squeezed my arm:

'But you made up for it, didn't you? And I'm so grateful that you did, otherwise I wouldn't have my Dan to love now.' I looked up at the compassion in her eyes:

'Yes, I suppose I did...'

'You did, Dad. And more than that, you've been a marvellous father to Dan. We both owe you so much, Dad.'

'Dad? What's this Dad business?' I looked up into Janey's eyes to see a puzzled smile on her face as she walked towards us across the bar, and reached out to take her hand as she eased into the chair beside me:

'It seems our boy has finally asked Steph if she's fool enough to marry him.'

'And you're daft enough to say yes?' She asked Steph in mock despair; the girl laughed:

'Well, I haven't actually told him yet...'

'Good for you, girl! Keep him in suspense' I told her.

'Keep who in suspense – are you talking about me, by any chance?' We all looked around as Daniel strode from the outer door. Stephanie got to her feet and gave him a tight hug and a kiss:

'Who else, darling?'

'And what's the suspense?' Janey was on her feet too, taking her son in her arms.

'I was just saying that I haven't actually agreed to marry you yet.' Steph replied; Dan looked at her in surprise:

'But you are going to – aren't you?'

'So presumptuous, this boy!' Steph addressed her comment to me, chuckling, as I shook my stepson by the hand. He drew me too into a hug, talking over my shoulder:

'You are going to, though?'

'Of course I am, stupid!' We all laughed as we returned to our seats and Dan drew up another chair.

'You know they've asked me to stay on and do post-grad research?' Janey and I both nodded: 'Well, I've agreed to do at least a year, 'til Steph finishes her degree, then we'll decide what we want to do after that.' Their hands met across the table, and Janey gave me a knowing smile:

'So when's the wedding?'

'Hold your horses, Mum! She's only just agreed to marry me!' Dan managed to look slightly scandalised. But Janey wasn't one to be put off:

'And have you talked about having children?'

'Mother!'

'Well, don't be too long about it, will you? I want some grandchildren, before I'm too old to enjoy them! So does your Dad.' Grandchildren! Of course I'd assumed Daniel would marry one day, and there would almost certainly be children, in time. He might not carry my genes, but he carried my name, so his children would be my grandchildren, too. I gazed across at him, and caught his smile in return: Dark grey eyes, tousled mid-brown hair, that frank, open face – I could almost have been looking at a grown-up Sammy; and now the Andrews name would go on, despite my own failure to produce children of my own.

Daniel seemed to sense my feelings; he reached over and took my hand in his:

'A grandson for you, Dad – how about that? One day soon, eh?'

'I love you, Dan.'

'I love you too, Dad.'

Starlight

I come out here every night. I like to sit here on my own on the lockgate beside the still waters of the old canal as evening turns slowly into night and the world falls silent around me. Just the gentle murmur of water, chuckling as it creeps past the quoins of the gate and trickles into the empty lock, making the quiet of twilight that much more intense by its presence.

My aloneness is of my own choosing. I know that I have only to say the word, to drop the least of hints, to be welcomed into the arms of my family – to be with my son and his lovely wife, enjoying the robust vitality of their two boys, or with one of my girls: Jenny, so full of quiet pride as her own daughter prepares to present me with my first great-grandson this side of Christmas, or Sarah, my youngest, the high-flyer in her elegant home with her fellow-lawyer husband. But at this time of day, in this place, I choose to be alone.

I have had a full life; but though that echoing emptiness from the days of my childhood has diminished in proportion, it is still there. Anything less would be a disloyalty to Jake, and the time we had together. So little time! Months, only; but in that short time he had become my companion, my friend – and yes, I suppose, my hero. Outcast himself, the son of the lock-keeper, a 'dirty boatee' to our other classmates, he had taken under his wing the frightened little city kid who was almost too scared to try to find a way of fitting in to his new, lonely village life. Now, I can look at that time, and remember. The world he knew is long gone now – working boats no longer ply the waterways, the boating families all dispersed onto the bank, their labours done, their cheery, hardworking, illiterate way of life vanished into the mists of the past. And now, I have come back – come home, to the cottage he shared with his father, where I spent so many carefree hours through that distant summer.

This was never my place. From the beginning, it was his place; even if for so short a time he was happy to allow me to share it with him it can never be truly mine. I remember nights like this, sitting here with him, gazing out along the New Bank to where the aqueduct carries the canal over the river so far below. I remember watching, as I do tonight, in silent wonder as the sky reflected in the still water darkens gradually from tones of rose and amber through shades of blue into the black of night, and each star slowly emerges into full view like a shy child creeping out from behind a door to stare at a stranger.

So many years. Almost fifty of them, since that awful day. And it took so many years before I found any kind of peace, before the nightmares would leave me alone. My parents must have suffered as much as I did, rushing to my side night after night as I woke screaming from dreams in which I shared with him that moment of awful terror as the irresistible momentum of the deep-loaded boat caught him against the lockside, in the very instant that he thrust me from the water into the arms of the boatman. I console myself with the thought that he must, he *had* to have lost consciousness instantly... But doubts still haunt me. And the dreams still come, if only rarely now.

And he knew. As he dived into the water intent on saving me from my own stupidity he must have known that his chances of getting out again in time were infinitesimal. But that was how our friendship worked – he knew also, as I knew, that I would have done the same for him. Closer than brothers could ever be – it is perhaps the greatest privilege of my life to have known friendship of that kind, and its greatest sadness to have lost it so soon. 'What if' is a purposeless expression – and yet it repeats and repeats in my mind as I gaze at the stars glittering in the still dark water, as I look to a distant horizon where I can see, inexorable if indeterminate, the end of my own life approaching.

So now I sit here alone as twilight gathers, as the autumn bats begin to fly, swooping, skimming low over the water to catch their evening feast. And I wonder – if he had not intervened, if he had left that fateful day to what I know was its pre-ordained course, would his children and grandchildren be somehow occupying the spaces left in the world by the absence of mine?

Most of all, I wonder – would *he* be sitting here now, in the silent starlight, wondering, and remembering...?

If you have enjoyed these stories by S G Miles, check out his 'Geoffrey Lewis' books as listed in the front of this one. All are available from our website:
www.sgmpublishing.co.uk

Many are now also available in e-book formats to suit all the popular e-readers, from your usual retailers